Benito Cereno

By Herman Melville

Adansonia
Press

Published in 2018

Logo art adapted from work by Bernard Gagnon

ISBN-13: 978-1-387-77149-3

First published in 1855

Benito Cereno

IN THE YEAR 1799, Captain Amasa Delano, of Duxbury, in
ssachusetts, commanding a large sealer and general trader, lay at anchor,
th a valuable cargo, in the harbour of St. Maria -- a small, desert, uninhabited
nd towards the southern extremity of the long coast of Chili. There he had
iched for water.

On the second day, not long after dawn, while lying in his berth, his mate
ne below, informing him that a strange sail was coming into the bay. Ships
·re then not so plenty in those waters as now. He rose, dressed, and went on
ck.

The morning was one peculiar to that coast. Everything was mute and calm;
erything grey. The sea, though undulated into long roods of swells, seemed
ed, and was sleeked at the surface like waved lead that has cooled and set in
e smelter's mould. The sky seemed a grey mantle. Flights of troubled grey
vl, kith and kin with flights of troubled grey vapours among which they were
xed, skimmed low and fitfully over the waters, as swallows over meadows
fore storms. Shadows present, foreshadowing deeper shadows to come.

To Captain Delano's surprise, the stranger, viewed through the glass, showed
colours; though to do so upon entering a haven, however uninhabited in its
ores, where but a single other ship might be lying, was the custom among
aceful seamen of all nations. Considering the lawlessness and loneliness of
e spot, and the sort of stories, at that day, associated with those seas, Captain
lano's surprise might have deepened into some uneasiness had he not been a
rson of a singularly undistrustful good nature, not liable, except on
.raordinary and repeated excitement, and hardly then, to indulge in personal
rms, any way involving the imputation of malign evil in man. Whether, in
w of what humanity is capable, such a trait implies, along with a benevolent
art, more than ordinary quickness and accuracy of intellectual perception,
·y be left to the wise to determine.

But whatever misgivings might have obtruded on first seeing the stranger
·uld almost, in any seaman's mind, have been dissipated by observing that
e ship, in navigating into the harbour, was drawing too near the land, for her
·n safety's sake, owing to a sunken reef making out off her bow. This seemed
prove her a stranger, indeed, not only to the sealer, but the island;
isequently, she could be no wonted freebooter on that ocean. With no small

interest, Captain Delano continued to watch her- a proceeding not much facilitated by the vapours partly mantling the hull, through which the far mati light from her cabin streamed equivocally enough; much like the sun- by this time crescented on the rim of the horizon, and apparently, in company with tl strange ship, entering the harbour- which, wimpled by the same low, creepin; clouds, showed not unlike a Lima intriguante's one sinister eye peering acros: the Plaza from the Indian loop-hole of her dusk *saya-y-manta*.

It might have been but a deception of the vapours, but, the longer the stranger was watched, the more singular appeared her manoeuvres. Ere long seemed hard to decide whether she meant to come in or no- what she wanted or what she was about. The wind, which had breezed up a little during the night, was now extremely light and baffling, which the more increased the apparent uncertainty of her movements.

Surmising, at last, that it might be a ship in distress, Captain Delano ordere his whale-boat to be dropped, and, much to the wary opposition of his mate, prepared to board her, and, at the least, pilot her in. On the night previous, a fishing-party of the seamen had gone a long distance to some detached rocks out of sight from the sealer, and, an hour or two before day-break, had returned, having met with no small success. Presuming that the stranger migl have been long off soundings, the good captain put several baskets of the fish, for presents, into his boat, and so pulled away. From her continuing too near the sunken reef, deeming her in danger, calling to his men, he made all haste t apprise those on board of their situation. But, some time ere the boat came uf the wind, light though it was, having shifted, had headed the vessel off, as wel as partly broken the vapours from about her.

Upon gaining a less remote view, the ship, when made signally visible on tk verge of the leaden-hued swells, with the shreds of fog here and there raggedi furring her, appeared like a whitewashed monastery after a thunder-storm, seen perched upon some dun cliff among the Pyrenees. But it was no purely fanciful resemblance which now, for a moment, almost led Captain Delano to think that nothing less than a ship-load of monks was before him. Peering ove the bulwarks were what really seemed, in the hazy distance, throngs of dark cowls; while, fitfully revealed through the open port-holes, other dark movin; figures were dimly descried, as of Black Friars pacing the cloisters.

Upon a still nigher approach, this appearance was modified, and the true character of the vessel was plain- a Spanish merchantman of the first class; carrying Negro slaves, amongst other valuable freight, from one colonial port another. A very large, and, in its time, a very fine vessel, such as in those days were at intervals encountered along that main; sometimes superseded Acapulco treasure-ships, or retired frigates of the Spanish king's navy, which, e superannuated Italian palaces, still, under a decline of masters, preserved ns of former state.

As the whale-boat drew more and more nigh, the cause of the peculiar pipe-yed aspect of the stranger was seen in the slovenly neglect pervading her. e spars, ropes, and great part of the bulwarks looked woolly, from long acquaintance with the scraper, tar, and the brush. Her keel seemed laid, her s put together, and she launched, from Ezekiel's Valley of Dry Bones.

In the present business in which she was engaged, the ship's general model d rig appeared to have undergone no material change from their original rlike and Froissart pattern. However, no guns were seen.

The tops were large, and were railed about with what had once been agonal net-work, all now in sad disrepair. These tops hung overhead like ee ruinous aviaries, in one of which was seen perched, on a ratlin, a white ddy, a strange fowl, so called from its lethargic somnambulistic character, ng frequently caught by hand at sea. Battered and mouldy, the castellated ecastle seemed some ancient turret, long ago taken by assault, and then left decay. Towards the stern, two high-raised quarter galleries- the balustrades e and there covered with dry, tindery sea-moss- opening out from the occupied state-cabin, whose dead lights, for all the mild weather, were metically closed and caulked- these tenantless balconies hung over the sea if it were the grand Venetian canal. But the principal relic of faded grandeur s the ample oval of the shield-like stern-piece, intricately carved with the ns of Castile and Leon, medallioned about by groups of mythological or nbolical devices; uppermost and central of which was a dark satyr in a mask, ding his foot on the prostrate neck of a writhing figure, likewise masked.

Whether the ship had a figure-head, or only a plain beak, was not quite tain, owing to canvas wrapped about that part, either to protect it while dergoing a refurbishing, or else decently to hide its decay. Rudely painted or lked, as in a sailor freak, along the forward side of a sort of pedestal below canvas, was the sentence, "Seguidvuestrojefe" (follow your leader); while n the tarnished head-boards, near by, appeared, in stately capitals, once gilt, ship's name, "SAN DOMINICK," each letter streakingly corroded with klings of copper-spike rust; while, like mourning weeds, dark festoons of -grass slimily swept to and fro over the name, with every hearse-like roll of hull.

As at last the boat was hooked from the bow along toward the gangway idship, its keel, while yet some inches separated from the hull, harshly ted as on a sunken coral reef. It proved a huge bunch of conglobated rnacles adhering below the water to the side like a wen; a token of baffling s and long calms passed somewhere in those seas.

Climbing the side, the visitor was at once surrounded by a clamorous thro
of whites and blacks, but the latter outnumbering the former more than coul
have been expected, Negro transportation-ship as the stranger in port was. B
in one language, and as with one voice, all poured out a common tale of
suffering; in which the Negresses, of whom there were not a few, exceeded th
others in their dolorous vehemence. The scurvy, together with a fever, had
swept off a great part of their number, more especially the Spaniards. Off Cap
Horn, they had narrowly escaped shipwreck; then, for days together, they had
lain tranced without wind; their provisions were low; their water next to non
their lips that moment were baked.

While Captain Delano was thus made the mark of all eager tongues, his one
eager glance took in all the faces, with every other object about him.

Always upon first boarding a large and populous ship at sea, especially a
foreign one, with a nondescript crew such as Lascars or Manilla men, the
impression varies in a peculiar way from that produced by first entering a
strange house with strange inmates in a strange land. Both house and ship, th
one by its walls and blinds, the other by its high bulwarks like ramparts, hoar
from view their interiors till the last moment; but in the case of the ship there
this addition: that the living spectacle it contains, upon its sudden and comple
disclosure, has, in contrast with the blank ocean which zones it, something of
the effect of enchantment. The ship seems unreal; these strange costumes,
gestures, and faces, but a shadowy tableau just emerged from the deep, which
directly must receive back what it gave.

Perhaps it was some such influence as above is attempted to be described
which, in Captain Delano's mind, heightened whatever, upon a staid scrutiny,
might have seemed unusual; especially the conspicuous figures of four elderly
grizzled Negroes, their heads like black, doddered willow tops, who, in
venerable contrast to the tumult below them, were couched sphynx-like, one
the starboard cat-head, another on the larboard, and the remaining pair face
face on the opposite bulwarks above the main-chains. They each had bits of
unstranded old junk in their hands, and, with a sort of stoical self-content, we
picking the junk into oakum, a small heap of which lay by their sides. They
accompanied the task with a continuous, low, monotonous chant; droning an
drooling away like so many grey-headed bag-pipers playing a funeral march.

The quarter-deck rose into an ample elevated poop, upon the forward verg
of which, lifted, like the oakum-pickers, some eight feet above the general
throng, sat along in a row, separated by regular spaces, the cross-legged figur
of six other blacks; each with a rusty hatchet in his hand, which, with a bit of
brick and a rag, he was engaged like a scullion in scouring; while between eac
two was a small stack of hatchets, their rusted edges turned forward awaiting
like operation. Though occasionally the four oakum-pickers would briefly

dress some person or persons in the crowd below, yet the six hatchet-
ishers neither spoke to others, nor breathed a whisper among themselves,
sat intent upon their task, except at intervals, when, with the peculiar love
Negroes of uniting industry with pastime, two-and-two they sideways
shed their hatchets together, like cymbals, with a barbarous din. All six,
like the generality, had the raw aspect of unsophisticated Africans.

But the first comprehensive glance which took in those ten figures, with
res less conspicuous, rested but an instant upon them, as, impatient of the
bub of voices, the visitor turned in quest of whomsoever it might be that
nmanded the ship.

But as if not unwilling to let nature make known her own case among his
fering charge, or else in despair of restraining it for the time, the Spanish
tain, a gentlemanly, reserved-looking, and rather young man to a stranger's
, dressed with singular richness, but bearing plain traces of recent sleepless
es and disquietudes, stood passively by, leaning against the main-mast, at
moment casting a dreary, spiritless look upon his excited people, at the
t an unhappy glance toward his visitor. By his side stood a black of small
ture, in whose rude face, as occasionally, like a shepherd's dog, he mutely
ned it up into the Spaniard's, sorrow and affection were equally blended.

Struggling through the throng, the American advanced to the Spaniard,
uring him of his sympathies, and offering to render whatever assistance
ght be in his power. To which the Spaniard returned, for the present, but
ve and ceremonious acknowledgments, his national formality dusked by the
urnine mood of ill health.

But losing no time in mere compliments, Captain Delano returning to the
gway, had his baskets of fish brought up; and as the wind still continued
t, so that some hours at least must elapse ere the ship could be brought to
 anchorage, he bade his men return to the sealer, and fetch back as much
ter as the whaleboat could carry, with whatever soft bread the steward
ght have, all the remaining pumpkins on board, with a box of sugar, and a
en of his private bottles of cider.

Not many minutes after the boat's pushing off, to the vexation of all, the wind
irely died away, and the tide turning, began drifting back the ship helplessly
ward. But trusting this would not last, Captain Delano sought with good
es to cheer up the strangers, feeling no small satisfaction that, with persons
heir condition he could- thanks to his frequent voyages along the Spanish
in- converse with some freedom in their native tongue.

While left alone with them, he was not long in observing some things tending
heighten his first impressions; but surprise was lost in pity, both for the
niards and blacks, alike evidently reduced from scarcity of water and
visions; while long-continued suffering seemed to have brought out the less

7

good-natured qualities of the Negroes, besides, at the same time, impairing th Spaniard's authority over them. But, under the circumstances, precisely this condition of things was to have been anticipated. In armies, navies, cities, or families- in nature herself- nothing more relaxes good order than misery. Stil Captain Delano was not without the idea, that had Benito Cereno been a man greater energy, misrule would hardly have come to the present pass. But the debility, constitutional or induced by the hardships, bodily and mental, of the Spanish captain, was too obvious to be overlooked. A prey to settled dejectio as if long mocked with hope he would not now indulge it, even when it had ceased to be a mock, the prospect of that day or evening at furthest, lying at anchor, with plenty of water for his people, and a brother captain to counsel and befriend, seemed in no perceptible degree to encourage him. His mind appeared unstrung, if not still more seriously affected. Shut up in these oaker walls, chained to one dull round of command, whose unconditionality cloyed him, like some hypochondriac abbot he moved slowly about, at times sudden pausing, starting, or staring, biting his lip, biting his finger-nail, flushing, palin twitching his beard, with other symptoms of an absent or moody mind. This distempered spirit was lodged, as before hinted, in as distempered a frame. F was rather tall, but seemed never to have been robust, and now with nervous suffering was almost worn to a skeleton. A tendency to some pulmonary complaint appeared to have been lately confirmed. His voice was like that of one with lungs half gone, hoarsely suppressed, a husky whisper. No wonder that, as in this state he tottered about, his private servant apprehensively followed him. Sometimes the Negro gave his master his arm, or took his handkerchief out of his pocket for him; performing these and similar offices with that affectionate zeal which transmutes into something filial or fraterna acts in themselves but menial; and which has gained for the Negro the repute making the most pleasing body-servant in the world; one, too, whom a maste need be on no stiffly superior terms with, but may treat with familiar trust; le a servant than a devoted companion.

Marking the noisy indocility of the blacks in general, as well as what seeme the sullen inefficiency of the whites, it was not without humane satisfaction t Captain Delano witnessed the steady good conduct of Babo.

But the good conduct of Babo, hardly more than the ill-behaviour of others seemed to withdraw the half-lunatic Don Benito from his cloudy languor. Not that such precisely was the impression made by the Spaniard on the mind of visitor. The Spaniard's individual unrest was, for the present, but noted as a conspicuous feature in the ship's general affliction. Still, Captain Delano was a little concerned at what he could not help taking for the time to be Don Benito's unfriendly indifference toward himself. The Spaniard's manner, too, conveyed a sort of sour and gloomy disdain, which he seemed at no pains to disguise. But this the American in charity ascribed to the harassing effects of

kness, since, in former instances, he had noted that there are peculiar
:ures on whom prolonged physical suffering seems to cancel every social
tinct of kindness; as if forced to black bread themselves, they deemed it but
uity that each person coming nigh them should, indirectly, by some slight or
ront, be made to partake of their fare.

But ere long Captain Delano bethought him that, indulgent as he was at the
st, in judging the Spaniard, he might not, after all, have exercised charity
ough. At bottom it was Don Benito's reserve which displeased him; but the
ne reserve was shown toward all but his personal attendant. Even the formal
oorts which, according to sea-usage, were at stated times made to him by
ne petty underling (either a white, mulatto or black), he hardly had patience
ough to listen to, without betraying contemptuous aversion. His manner
on such occasions was, in its degree, not unlike that which might be
oposed to have been his imperial countryman's, Charles V., just previous to
: anchoritish retirement of that monarch from the throne.

This splenetic disrelish of his place was evinced in almost every function
rtaining to it. Proud as he was moody, he condescended to no personal
indate. Whatever special orders were necessary, their delivery was delegated
his body-servant, who in turn transferred them to their ultimate destination,
ough runners, alert Spanish boys or slave boys, like pages or pilot-fish within
sy call continually hovering round Don Benito. So that to have beheld this
demonstrative invalid gliding about, apathetic and mute, no landsman could
ve dreamed that in him was lodged a dictatorship beyond which, while at sea,
re was no earthly appeal.

Thus, the Spaniard, regarded in his reserve, seemed as the involuntary victim
mental disorder. But, in fact, his reserve might, in some degree, have
oceeded from design. If so, then in Don Benito was evinced the unhealthy
nax of that icy though conscientious policy, more or less adopted by all
nmanders of large ships, which, except in signal emergencies, obliterates
ke the manifestation of sway with every trace of sociality; transforming the
n into a block, or rather into a loaded cannon, which, until there is call for
under, has nothing to say.

Viewing him in this light, it seemed but a natural token of the perverse habit
luced by a long course of such hard self-restraint, that, notwithstanding the
esent condition of his ship, the Spaniard should still persist in a demeanour,
ich, however harmless- or it may be, appropriate- in a well-appointed vessel,
ch as the San Dominick might have been at the outset of the voyage, was
ything but judicious now. But the Spaniard perhaps thought that it was with
otains as with gods: reserve, under all events, must still be their cue. But
re probably this appearance of slumbering dominion might have been but an
empted disguise to conscious imbecility- not deep policy, but shallow device.

But be all this as it might, whether Don Benito's manner was designed or not, the more Captain Delano noted its pervading reserve, the less he felt uneasine at any particular manifestation of that reserve toward himself.

Neither were his thoughts taken up by the captain alone. Wonted to the qu orderliness of the sealer's comfortable family of a crew, the noisy confusion o the San Dominick's suffering host repeatedly challenged his eye. Some prominent breaches not only of discipline but of decency were observed. The Captain Delano could not but ascribe, in the main, to the absence of those subordinate deck-officers to whom, along with higher duties, is entrusted wh may be styled the police department of a populous ship. True, the old oakum-pickers appeared at times to act the part of monitorial constables to their countrymen, the blacks; but though occasionally succeeding in allaying triflin outbreaks now and then between man and man, they could do little or nothin toward establishing general quiet. The San Dominick was in the condition of a transatlantic emigrant ship, among whose multitude of living freight are som individuals, doubtless, as little troublesome as crates and bales; but the frienc remonstrances of such with their ruder companions are of not so much avail a the unfriendly arm of the mate. What the San Dominick wanted was, what the emigrant ship has, stern superior officers. But on these decks not so much as a fourth mate was to be seen.

The visitor's curiosity was roused to learn the particulars of those mishaps which had brought about such absenteeism, with its consequences; because, though deriving some inkling of the voyage from the wails which at the first moment had greeted him, yet of the details no clear understanding had been had. The best account would, doubtless, be given by the captain. Yet at first th visitor was loth to ask it, unwilling to provoke some distant rebuff. But plucki up courage, he at last accosted Don Benito, renewing the expression of his benevolent interest, adding, that did he (Captain Delano) but know the particulars of the ship's misfortunes, he would, perhaps, be better able in the end to relieve them. Would Don Benito favour him with the whole story?

Don Benito faltered; then, like some somnambulist suddenly interfered wit vacantly stared at his visitor, and ended by looking down on the deck. He maintained this posture so long, that Captain Delano, almost equally disconcerted, and involuntarily almost as rude, turned suddenly from him, walking forward to accost one of the Spanish seamen for the desired information. But he had hardly gone five paces, when with a sort of eagerness Don Benito invited him back, regretting his momentary absence of mind, and professing readiness to gratify him.

While most part of the story was being given, the two captains stood on the after part of the main-deck, a privileged spot, no one being near but the serva

"It is now a hundred and ninety days," began the Spaniard, in his husky isper, "that this ship, well officered and well manned, with several cabin ssengers- some fifty Spaniards in all- sailed from Buenos Ayres bound to ia, with a general cargo, Paraguay tea and the like- and," pointing forward, at parcel of Negroes, now not more than a hundred and fifty, as you see, but n numbering over three hundred souls. Off Cape Horn we had heavy gales. In e moment, by night, three of my best officers, with fifteen sailors, were lost, h the main-yard; the spar snapping under them in the slings, as they sought, h heavers, to beat down the icy sail. To lighten the hull, the heavier sacks of ta were thrown into the sea, with most of the water-pipes lashed on deck at time. And this last necessity it was, combined with the prolonged detentions erwards experienced, which eventually brought about our chief causes of fering. When-"

Here there was a sudden fainting attack of his cough, brought on, no doubt, his mental distress. His servant sustained him, and drawing a cordial from pocket placed it to his lips. He a little revived. But unwilling to leave him supported while yet imperfectly restored, the black with one arm still circled his master, at the same time keeping his eye fixed on his face, as if to tch for the first sign of complete restoration, or relapse, as the event might ove.

The Spaniard proceeded, but brokenly and obscurely, as one in a dream.

-"Oh, my God! Rather than pass through what I have, with joy I would have led the most terrible gales; but-"

His cough returned and with increased violence; this subsiding, with Idened lips and closed eyes he fell heavily against his supporter.

"His mind wanders. He was thinking of the plague that followed the gales," intively sighed the servant; "my poor, poor master!" wringing one hand, and h the other wiping the mouth. "But be patient, Senor," again turning to otain Delano, "these fits do not last long; master will soon be himself."

Don Benito reviving, went on; but as this portion of the story was very okenly delivered, the substance only will here be set down.

t appeared that after the ship had been many days tossed in storms off the oe, the scurvy broke out, carrying off numbers of the whites and blacks. ien at last they had worked round into the Pacific, their spars and sails were damaged, and so inadequately handled by the surviving mariners, most of om were become invalids, that, unable to lay her northerly course by the id, which was powerful, the unmanageable ship for successive days and hts was blown northwestward, where the breeze suddenly deserted her, in known waters, to sultry calms. The absence of the water-pipes now proved fatal to life as before their presence had menaced it. Induced, or at least

11

aggravated, by the more than scanty allowance of water, a malignant fever followed the scurvy; with the excessive heat of the lengthened calm, making such short work of it as to sweep away, as by billows, whole families of the Africans, and a yet larger number, proportionally, of the Spaniards, including, by a luckless fatality, every officer on board. Consequently, in the smart west winds eventually following the calm, the already rent sails having to be simpl dropped, not furled, at need, had been gradually reduced to the beggar's rags they were now. To procure substitutes for his lost sailors, as well as supplies water and sails, the captain at the earliest opportunity had made for Baldivia, the southermost civilized port of Chili and South America; but upon nearing t coast the thick weather had prevented him from so much as sighting that harbour. Since which period, almost without a crew, and almost without canv and almost without water, and at intervals giving its added dead to the sea, tl San Dominick had been battle-dored about by contrary winds, inveigled by currents, or grown weedy in calms. Like a man lost in woods, more than once she had doubled upon her own track.

"But throughout these calamities," huskily continued Don Benito, painfully turning in the half embrace of his servant, "I have to thank those Negroes you see, who, though to your inexperienced eyes appearing unruly, have, indeed, conducted themselves with less of restlessness than even their owner could have thought possible under such circumstances."

Here he again fell faintly back. Again his mind wandered: but he rallied, an less obscurely proceeded.

"Yes, their owner was quite right in assuring me that no fetters would be needed with his blacks; so that while, as is wont in this transportation, those Negroes have always remained upon deck- not thrust below, as in the Guineamen- they have, also, from the beginning, been freely permitted to ran within given bounds at their pleasure."

Once more the faintness returned- his mind roved- but, recovering, he resumed:

"But it is Babo here to whom, under God, I owe not only my own preservation, but likewise to him, chiefly, the merit is due, of pacifying his mo ignorant brethren, when at intervals tempted to murmurings."

"Ah, master," sighed the black, bowing his face, "don't speak of me; Babo is nothing; what Babo has done was but duty."

"Faithful fellow!" cried Captain Delano. "Don Benito, I envy you such a frier slave I cannot call him."

As master and man stood before him, the black upholding the white, Capta Delano could not but bethink him of the beauty of that relationship which cou present such a spectacle of fidelity on the one hand and confidence on the

er. The scene was heightened by the contrast in dress, denoting their
ative positions. The Spaniard wore a loose Chili jacket of dark velvet; white
all clothes and stockings, with silver buckles at the knee and instep; a high-
wned sombrero, of fine grass; a slender sword, silver mounted, hung from a
t in his sash; the last being an almost invariable adjunct, more for utility
n ornament, of a South American gentleman's dress to this hour. Excepting
en his occasional nervous contortions brought about disarray, there was a
tain precision in his attire, curiously at variance with the unsightly disorder
und; especially in the belittered Ghetto, forward of the main-mast, wholly
upied by the blacks.

he servant wore nothing but wide trousers, apparently, from their
rseness and patches, made out of some old top-sail; they were clean, and
fined at the waist by a bit of unstranded rope, which, with his composed,
recatory air at times, made him look something like a begging friar of St.
ncis.

owever unsuitable for the time and place, at least in the blunt thinking
erican's eyes, and however strangely surviving in the midst of all his
ictions, the toilette of Don Benito might not, in fashion at least, have gone
ond the style of the day among South Americans of his class. Though on the
sent voyage sailing from Buenos Ayres, he had avowed himself a native and
ident of Chili, whose inhabitants had not so generally adopted the plain coat
once plebeian pantaloons; but, with a becoming modification, adhered to
ir provincial costume, picturesque as any in the world. Still, relatively to the
e history of the voyage, and his own pale face, there seemed something so
ongruous in the Spaniard's apparel, as almost to suggest the image of an
alid courtier tottering about London streets in the time of the plague.

he portion of the narrative which, perhaps, most excited interest, as well as
ne surprise, considering the latitudes in question, was the long calms spoken
and more particularly the ship's so long drifting about. Without
nmunicating the opinion, of course, the American could not but impute at
st part of the detentions both to clumsy seamanship and faulty navigation.
ing Don Benito's small, yellow hands, he easily inferred that the young
tain had not got into command at the hawse-hole but the cabin-window, and
, why wonder at incompetence, in youth, sickness, and aristocracy united?
h was his democratic conclusion.

But drowning criticism in compassion, after a fresh repetition of his
npathies, Captain Delano having heard out his story, not only engaged, as in
first place, to see Don Benito and his people supplied in their immediate
lily needs, but, also, now further promised to assist him in procuring a large
manent supply of water, as well as some sails and rigging; and, though it
uld involve no small embarrassment to himself, yet he would spare three of

13

his best seamen for temporary deck officers; so that without delay the ship might proceed to Concepcion, there fully to refit for Lima, her destined port.

Such generosity was not without its effect, even upon the invalid. His face lighted up; eager and hectic, he met the honest glance of his visitor. With gratitude he seemed overcome.

"This excitement is bad for master," whispered the servant, taking his arm and with soothing words gently drawing him aside.

When Don Benito returned, the American was pained to observe that his hopefulness, like the sudden kindling in his cheek, was but febrile and transie

Ere long, with a joyless mien, looking up toward the poop, the host invited his guest to accompany him there, for the benefit of what little breath of winc might be stirring.

As during the telling of the story, Captain Delano had once or twice started the occasional cymballing of the hatchet-polishers, wondering why such an interruption should be allowed, especially in that part of the ship, and in the ears of an invalid; and, moreover, as the hatchets had anything but an attract look, and the handlers of them still less so, it was, therefore, to tell the truth, without some lurking reluctance, or even shrinking, it may be, that Captain Delano, with apparent complaisance, acquiesced in his host's invitation. The more so, since with an untimely caprice of punctilio, rendered distressing by cadaverous aspect, Don Benito, with Castilian bows, solemnly insisted upon l guest's preceding him up the ladder leading to the elevation; where, one on each side of the last step, sat four armorial supporters and sentries, two of th ominous file. Gingerly enough stepped good Captain Delano between them, a in the instant of leaving them behind, like one running the gauntlet, he felt an apprehensive twitch in the calves of his legs

But when, facing about, he saw the whole file, like so many organ-grinders still stupidly intent on their work, unmindful of everything beside, he could n but smile at his late fidgeting panic.

Presently, while standing with Don Benito, looking forward upon the deck below, he was struck by one of those instances of insubordination previously alluded to. Three black boys, with two Spanish boys, were sitting together on the hatches, scraping a rude wooden platter, in which some scanty mess had recently been cooked. Suddenly, one of the black boys, enraged at a word dropped by one of his white companions, seized a knife, and though called to forbear by one of the oakum-pickers, struck the lad over the head, inflicting a gash from which blood flowed.

In amazement, Captain Delano inquired what this meant. To which the pal Benito dully muttered, that it was merely the sport of the lad.

14

'Pretty serious sport, truly," rejoined Captain Delano. "Had such a thing opened on board the Bachelor's Delight, instant punishment would have followed."

At these words the Spaniard turned upon the American one of his sudden, ring, half-lunatic looks; then, relapsing into his torpor, answered, "Doubtless, doubtless, Senor."

Is it, thought Captain Delano, that this helpless man is one of those paper captains I've known, who by policy wink at what by power they cannot put down? I know no sadder sight than a commander who has little of command but the name.

'I should think, Don Benito," he now said, glancing toward the oakum-picker who had sought to interfere with the boys, "that you would find it advantageous to keep all your blacks employed, especially the younger ones, no matter at what useless task, and no matter what happens to the ship. Why, even with my little band, I find such a course indispensable. I once kept a crew on my quarterdeck thrumming mats for my cabin, when, for three days, I had given up my ship- mats, men, and all- for a speedy loss, owing to the violence of a gale in which we could do nothing but helplessly drive before it."

"Doubtless, doubtless," muttered Don Benito.

"But," continued Captain Delano, again glancing upon the oakum-pickers and then at the hatchet-polishers, near by, "I see you keep some at least of your host employed."

"Yes," was again the vacant response.

"Those old men there, shaking their pows from their pulpits," continued Captain Delano, pointing to the oakum-pickers, "seem to act the part of old monies to the rest, little heeded as their admonitions are at times. Is this voluntary on their part, Don Benito, or have you appointed them shepherds to your flock of black sheep?"

"What posts they fill, I appointed them," rejoined the Spaniard in an acrid tone, as if resenting some supposed satiric reflection.

"And these others, these Ashantee conjurors here," continued Captain Delano, rather uneasily eyeing the brandished steel of the hatchet-polishers, where in spots it had been brought to a shine, "this seems a curious business they are at, Don Benito?"

"In the gales we met," answered the Spaniard, "what of our general cargo was not thrown overboard was much damaged by the brine. Since coming into calm weather, I have had several cases of knives and hatchets daily brought up for overhauling and cleaning."

15

"A prudent idea, Don Benito. You are part owner of ship and cargo, I presume; but not of the slaves, perhaps?"

"I am owner of all you see," impatiently returned Don Benito, "except the main company of blacks, who belonged to my late friend, AlexandroAranda."

As he mentioned this name, his air was heart-broken, his knees shook; his servant supported him.

Thinking he divined the cause of such unusual emotion, to confirm his surmise, Captain Delano, after a pause, said, "And may I ask, Don Benito, whether- since awhile ago you spoke of some cabin passengers- the friend, whose loss so afflicts you, at the outset of the voyage accompanied his blacks"

"Yes."

"But died of the fever?"

"Died of the fever.- Oh, could I but-"

Again quivering, the Spaniard paused.

"Pardon me," said Captain Delano slowly, "but I think that, by a sympatheti experience, I conjecture, Don Benito, what it is that gives the keener edge to your grief. It was once my hard fortune to lose at sea a dear friend, my own brother, then supercargo. Assured of the welfare of his spirit, its departure I could have borne like a man; but that honest eye, that honest hand- both of which had so often met mine- and that warm heart; all, all- like scraps to the dogs- to throw all to the sharks! It was then I vowed never to have for fellow-voyager a man I loved, unless, unbeknown to him, I had provided every requisite, in case of a fatality, for embalming his mortal part for interment on shore. Were your friend's remains now on board this ship, Don Benito, not th strangely would the mention of his name affect you."

"On board this ship?" echoed the Spaniard. Then, with horrified gestures, a directed against some spectre, he unconsciously fell into the ready arms of hi attendant, who, with a silent appeal toward Captain Delano, seemed beseechi him not again to broach a theme so unspeakably distressing to his master.

This poor fellow now, thought the pained American, is the victim of that sa superstition which associates goblins with the deserted body of man, as ghos with an abandoned house. How unlike are we made! What to me, in like case, would have been a solemn satisfaction, the bare suggestion, even, terrifies the Spaniard into this trance. Poor AlexandroAranda! what would you say could you see your friend- who, on former voyages, when you for months were left behind, has, I dare say, often longed, and longed, for one peep at you- now transported with terror at the least thought of having you anyway nigh him.

16

At this moment, with a dreary graveyard toll, betokening a flaw, the ship's
ecastle bell, smote by one of the grizzled oakum-pickers, proclaimed ten
lock through the leaden calm; when Captain Delano's attention was caught
the moving figure of a gigantic black, emerging from the general crowd
ow, and slowly advancing toward the elevated poop. An iron collar was
ut his neck, from which depended a chain, thrice wound round his body; the
minating links padlocked together at a broad band of iron, his girdle.

'How like a mute Atufal moves," murmured the servant.

The black mounted the steps of the poop, and, like a brave prisoner, brought
to receive sentence, stood in unquailing muteness before Don Benito, now
overed from his attack.

At the first glimpse of his approach, Don Benito had started, a resentful
dow swept over his face; and, as with the sudden memory of bootless rage,
white lips glued together.

This is some mulish mutineer, thought Captain Delano, surveying, not
hout a mixture of admiration, the colossal form of the Negro.

'See, he waits your question, master," said the servant.

Thus reminded, Don Benito, nervously averting his glance, as if shunning, by
icipation, some rebellious response, in a disconcerted voice, thus spoke:

'Atufal, will you ask my pardon now?"

The black was silent.

'Again, master," murmured the servant, with bitter upbraiding eyeing his
ntryman. "Again, master; he will bend to master yet."

'Answer," said Don Benito, still averting his glance, "say but the one word
·don, and your chains shall be off."

Upon this, the black, slowly raising both arms, let them lifelessly fall, his links
nking, his head bowed; as much as to say, "No, I am content."

'Go," said Don Benito, with inkept and unknown emotion.

Deliberately as he had come, the black obeyed.

'Excuse me, Don Benito," said Captain Delano, "but this scene surprises me;
at means it, pray?"

'It means that that Negro alone, of all the band, has given me peculiar cause
offence. I have put him in chains; I --"

Here he paused; his hand to his head, as if there were a swimming there, or a
den bewilderment of memory had come over him; but meeting his servant's
dly glance seemed reassured, and proceeded:

17

"I could not scourge such a form. But I told him he must ask my pardon. As yet he has not. At my command, every two hours he stands before me."

"And how long has this been?"

"Some sixty days."

"And obedient in all else?And respectful?"

"Yes."

"Upon my conscience, then," exclaimed Captain Delano, impulsively, "he ha a royal spirit in him, this fellow."

"He may have some right to it," bitterly returned Don Benito; "he says he w king in his own land."

"Yes," said the servant, entering a word, "those slits in Atufal's ears once he wedges of gold; but poor Babo here, in his own land, was only a poor slave; a black man's slave wasBabo, who now is the white's."

Somewhat annoyed by these conversational familiarities, Captain Delano turned curiously upon the attendant, then glanced inquiringly at his master; but, as if long wonted to these little informalities, neither master nor man seemed to understand him.

"What, pray, was Atufal's offence, Don Benito?" asked Captain Delano; "if it was not something very serious, take a fool's advice, and, in view of his gener docility, as well as in some natural respect for his spirit, remit his penalty."

"No, no, master never will do that," here murmured the servant to himself, "proud Atufal must first ask master's pardon. The slave there carries the padlock, but master here carries the key."

His attention thus directed, Captain Delano now noticed for the first time that, suspended by a slender silken cord, from Don Benito's neck hung a key. once, from the servant's muttered syllables divining the key's purpose, he smiled and said: "So, Don Benito- padlock and key- significant symbols, truly.

Biting his lip, Don Benito faltered.

Though the remark of Captain Delano, a man of such native simplicity as tc be incapable of satire or irony, had been dropped in playful allusion to the Spaniard's singularly evidenced lordship over the black; yet the hypochondri seemed in some way to have taken it as a malicious reflection upon his confessed inability thus far to break down, at least, on a verbal summons, the entrenched will of the slave. Deploring this supposed misconception, yet despairing of correcting it, Captain Delano shifted the subject; but finding his companion more than ever withdrawn, as if still slowly digesting the lees of tl presumed affront above-mentioned, by-and-by Captain Delano likewise beca

talkative, oppressed, against his own will, by what seemed the secret
dictiveness of the morbidly sensitive Spaniard. But the good sailor himself,
quite contrary disposition, refrained, on his part, alike from the appearance
rom the feeling of resentment, and if silent, was only so from contagion.

Presently the Spaniard, assisted by his servant, somewhat discourteously
ssed over from Captain Delano; a procedure which, sensibly enough, might
e been allowed to pass for idle caprice of ill-humour, had not master and
n, lingering round the corner of the elevated skylight, begun whispering
ether in low voices. This was unpleasing. And more: the moody air of the
niard, which at times had not been without a sort of valetudinarian
teliness, now seemed anything but dignified; while the menial familiarity of
servant lost its original charm of simple-hearted attachment.

n his embarrassment, the visitor turned his face to the other side of the ship.
so doing, his glance accidentally fell on a young Spanish sailor, a coil of rope
his hand, just stepped from the deck to the first round of the mizzen-rigging.
haps the man would not have been particularly noticed, were it not that,
ing his ascent to one of the yards, he, with a sort of covert intentness, kept
eye fixed on Captain Delano, from whom, presently, it passed, as if by a
ural sequence, to the two whisperers.

His own attention thus redirected to that quarter, Captain Delano gave a
ht start. From something in Don Benito's manner just then, it seemed as if
visitor had, at least partly, been the subject of the withdrawn consultation
ng on- a conjecture as little agreeable to the guest as it was little flattering to
host.

The singular alternations of courtesy and ill-breeding in the Spanish captain
re unaccountable, except on one of two suppositions- innocent lunacy, or
ked imposture.

But the first idea, though it might naturally have occurred to an indifferent
erver, and, in some respects, had not hitherto been wholly a stranger to
tain Delano's mind, yet, now that, in an incipient way, he began to regard
stranger's conduct something in the light of an intentional affront, of course
idea of lunacy was virtually vacated. But if not a lunatic, what then? Under
circumstances, would a gentleman, nay, any honest boor, act the part now
ed by his host? The man was an impostor. Some lowborn adventurer,
squerading as an oceanic grandee; yet so ignorant of the first requisites of
re gentlemanhood as to be betrayed into the present remarkable indecorum.
t strange ceremoniousness, too, at other times evinced, seemed not
haracteristic of one playing a part above his real level. Benito Cereno- Don
ito Cereno- a sounding name. One, too, at that period, not unknown, in the
name, to supercargoes and sea captains trading along the Spanish Main, as
onging to one of the most enterprising and extensive mercantile families in

all those provinces; several members of it having titles; a sort of Castilian Rothschild, with a noble brother, or cousin, in every great trading town of So America. The alleged Don Benito was in early manhood, about twenty-nine o thirty. To assume a sort of roving cadetship in the maritime affairs of such a house, what more likely scheme for a young knave of talent and spirit? But th Spaniard was a pale invalid. Never mind. For even to the degree of simulating mortal disease, the craft of some tricksters had been known to attain. To thin that, under the aspect of infantile weakness, the most savage energies might ' couched- those velvets of the Spaniard but the velvet paw to his fangs.

From no train of thought did these fancies come; not from within, but from without; suddenly, too, and in one throng, like hoar frost; yet as soon to vanis as the mild sun of Captain Delano's good-nature regained its meridian.

Glancing over once again toward Don Benito- whose side-face, revealed above the skylight, was now turned toward him- Captain Delano was struck l the profile, whose clearness of cut was refined by the thinness incident to ill-health, as well as ennobled about the chin by the beard. Away with suspicion. He was a true off-shoot of a true hidalgo Cereno.

Relieved by these and other better thoughts, the visitor, lightly humming a tune, now began indifferently pacing the poop, so as not to betray to Don Ber that be had at all mistrusted incivility, much less duplicity; for such mistrust would yet be proved illusory, and by the event; though, for the present, the circumstance which had provoked that distrust remained unexplained. But when that little mystery should have been cleared up, Captain Delano though he might extremely regret it, did he allow Don Benito to become aware that h had indulged in ungenerous surmises. In short, to the Spaniard's black-letter text, it was best, for a while, to leave open margin.

Presently, his pale face twitching and overcast, the Spaniard, still supporte by his attendant, moved over toward his guest, when, with even more than usual embarrassment, and a strange sort of intriguing intonation in his husky whisper, the following conversation began:

"Senor, may I ask how long you have lain at this isle?"

"Oh, but a day or two, Don Benito."

"And from what port are you last?"

"Canton."

"And there, Senor, you exchanged your seal-skins for teas and silks, I think you said?"

"Yes. Silks, mostly."

"And the balance you took in specie, perhaps?"

Captain Delano, fidgeting a little, answered-

"Yes; some silver; not a very great deal, though."

"Ah- well. May I ask how many men have you on board, Senor?"

Captain Delano slightly started, but answered:

"About five-and-twenty, all told."

"And at present, Senor, all on board, I suppose?"

"All on board, Don Benito," replied the captain now with satisfaction.

"And will be to-night, Senor?"

At this last question, following so many pertinacious ones, for the soul of him
ptain Delano could not but look very earnestly at the questioner, who,
tead of meeting the glance, with every token of craven discomposure
pped his eyes to the deck; presenting an unworthy contrast to his servant,
o, just then, was kneeling at his feet adjusting a loose shoe-buckle; his
engaged face meantime, with humble curiosity, turned openly up into his
ster's downcast one.

The Spaniard, still with a guilty shuffle, repeated his question:

"And- and will be to-night, Senor?"

"Yes, for aught I know," returned Captain Delano,- "but nay," rallying himself
o fearless truth, "some of them talked of going off on another fishing party
ut midnight."

"Your ships generally go- go more or less armed, I believe, Senor?"

"Oh, a six-pounder or two, in case of emergency," was the intrepidly
ifferent reply, "with a small stock of muskets, sealing-spears, and cutlasses,
u know."

As he thus responded, Captain Delano again glanced at Don Benito, but the
ter's eyes were averted; while abruptly and awkwardly shifting the subject,
made some peevish allusion to the calm, and then, without apology, once
re, with his attendant, withdrew to the opposite bulwarks, where the
ispering was resumed.

At this moment, and ere Captain Delano could cast a cool thought upon what
d just passed, the young Spanish sailor before mentioned was seen
scending from the rigging. In act of stooping over to spring inboard to the
ck, his voluminous, unconfined frock, or shirt, of coarse woollen, much
tted with tar, opened out far down the chest, revealing a soiled under-
ment of what seemed the finest linen, edged, about the neck, with a narrow
e ribbon, sadly faded and worn. At this moment the young sailor's eye was

again fixed on the whisperers, and Captain Delano thought he observed a lurking significance in it, as if silent signs of some freemason sort had that instant been interchanged.

This once more impelled his own glance in the direction of Don Benito, and as before, he could not but infer that himself formed the subject of the conference. He paused. The sound of the hatchet-polishing fell on his ears. He cast another swift side-look at the two. They had the air of conspirators. In connection with the late questionings, and the incident of the young sailor, these things now begat such return of involuntary suspicion, that the singular guilelessness of the American could not endure it. Plucking up a gay and humorous expression, he crossed over to the two rapidly, saying: "Ha, Don Benito, your black here seems high in your trust; a sort of privy-counsellor, in fact."

Upon this, the servant looked up with a good-natured grin, but the master started as from a venomous bite. It was a moment or two before the Spaniard sufficiently recovered himself to reply; which he did, at last, with cold constraint: "Yes, Senor, I have trust in Babo."

Here Babo, changing his previous grin of mere animal humour into an intelligent smile, not ungratefully eyed his master.

Finding that the Spaniard now stood silent and reserved, as if involuntarily or purposely giving hint that his guest's proximity was inconvenient just then Captain Delano, unwilling to appear uncivil even to incivility itself, made som trivial remark and moved off; again and again turning over in his mind the mysterious demeanour of Don Benito Cereno.

He had descended from the poop, and, wrapped in thought, was passing ne a dark hatchway, leading down into the steerage, when, perceiving motion there, he looked to see what moved. The same instant there was a sparkle in t shadowy hatchway, and he saw one of the Spanish sailors, prowling there, hurriedly placing his hand in the bosom of his frock, as if hiding something. Before the man could have been certain who it was that was passing, he slunk below out of sight. But enough was seen of him to make it sure that he was th same young sailor before noticed in the rigging.

What was that which so sparkled? thought Captain Delano. It was no lamp- no match- no live coal. Could it have been a jewel? But how come sailors with jewels?- or with silk-trimmed undershirts either? Has he been robbing the trunks of the dead cabin passengers? But if so, he would hardly wear one of th stolen articles on board ship here. Ah, ah- if now that was, indeed, a secret sig saw passing between this suspicious fellow and his captain awhile since; if I could only be certain that in my uneasiness my senses did not deceive me, the

Here, passing from one suspicious thing to another, his mind revolved the
nt of the strange questions put to him concerning his ship.

By a curious coincidence, as each point was recalled, the black wizards of
nantee would strike up with their hatchets, as in ominous comment on the
ite stranger's thoughts. Pressed by such enigmas and portents, it would have
en almost against nature, had not, even into the least distrustful heart, some
y misgivings obtruded.

Observing the ship now helplessly fallen into a current, with enchanted sails,
fting with increased rapidity seaward; and noting that, from a lately
ercepted projection of the land, the sealer was hidden, the stout mariner
gan to quake at thoughts which he barely durst confess to himself. Above all,
began to feel a ghostly dread of Don Benito. And yet when he roused himself,
ated his chest, felt himself strong on his legs, and coolly considered it- what
all these phantoms amount to?

Had the Spaniard any sinister scheme, it must have reference not so much to
n (Captain Delano) as to his ship (the Bachelor's Delight). Hence the present
fting away of the one ship from the other, instead of favouring any such
ssible scheme, was, for the time at least, opposed to it. Clearly any suspicion,
nbining such contradictions, must need be delusive. Beside, was it not
urd to think of a vessel in distress- a vessel by sickness almost dismanned of
crew- a vessel whose inmates were parched for water- was it not a
ousand times absurd that such a craft should, at present, be of a piratical
aracter; or her commander, either for himself or those under him, cherish
desire but for speedy relief and refreshment? But then, might not general
tress, and thirst in particular, be affected? And might not that same
diminished Spanish crew, alleged to have perished off to a remnant, be at
t very moment lurking in the hold? On heart-broken pretence of entreating a
of cold water, fiends in human form had got into lonely dwellings, nor
ired until a dark deed had been done. And among the Malay pirates, it was no
usual thing to lure ships after them into their treacherous harbours, or entice
arders from a declared enemy at sea, by the spectacle of thinly manned or
ant decks, beneath which prowled a hundred spears with yellow arms ready
upthrust them through the mats. Not that Captain Delano had entirely
dited such things. He had heard of them- and now, as stories, they recurred.
e present destination of the ship was the anchorage. There she would be near
own vessel. Upon gaining that vicinity, might not the San Dominick, like a
mbering volcano, suddenly let loose energies now hid?

He recalled the Spaniard's manner while telling his story. There was a
omy hesitancy and subterfuge about it. It was just the manner of one making
his tale for evil purposes, as he goes. But if that story was not true, what was
truth? That the ship had unlawfully come into the Spaniard's possession?

23

But in many of its details, especially in reference to the more calamitous parts such as the fatalities among the seamen, the consequent prolonged beating about, the past sufferings from obstinate calms, and still continued suffering from thirst; in all these points, as well as others, Don Benito's story had been corroborated not only by the wailing ejaculations of the indiscriminate multitude, white and black, but likewise- what seemed impossible to be counterfeit- by the very expression and play of every human feature, which Captain Delano saw. If Don Benito's story was throughout an invention, then every soul on board, down to the youngest Negress, was his carefully drilled recruit in the plot: an incredible inference. And yet, if there was ground for mistrusting the Spanish captain's veracity, that inference was a legitimate one.

In short, scarce an uneasiness entered the honest sailor's mind but, by a subsequent spontaneous act of good sense, it was ejected. At last he began to laugh at these forebodings; and laugh at the strange ship for, in its aspect someway siding with them, as it were; and laugh, too, at the odd-looking black particularly those old scissors-grinders, the Ashantees; and those bed-ridden old knitting-women, the oakum-pickers; and, in a human way, he almost began to laugh at the dark Spaniard himself, the central hobgoblin of all.

For the rest, whatever in a serious way seemed enigmatical, was now good naturedly explained away by the thought that, for the most part, the poor invalid scarcely knew what he was about; either sulking in black vapours, or putting random questions without sense or object. Evidently, for the present, the man was not fit to be entrusted with the ship. On some benevolent plea withdrawing the command from him, Captain Delano would yet have to send her to Concepcion in charge of his second mate, a worthy person and good navigator- a plan which would prove no wiser for the San Dominick than for Don Benito; for- relieved from all anxiety, keeping wholly to his cabin- the sic man, under the good nursing of his servant, would probably, by the end of the passage, be in a measure restored to health and with that he should also be restored to authority.

Such were the American's thoughts. They were tranquillizing. There was a difference between the idea of Don Benito's darkly preordaining Captain Delano's fate, and Captain Delano's lightly arranging Don Benito's. Nevertheless, it was not without something of relief that the good seaman presently perceived his whale-boat in the distance. Its absence had been prolonged by unexpected detention at the sealer's side, as well as its returning trip lengthened by the continual recession of the goal.

The advancing speck was observed by the blacks. Their shouts attracted the attention of Don Benito, who, with a return of courtesy, approaching Captain Delano, expressed satisfaction at the coming of some supplies, slight and temporary as they must necessarily prove.

24

Captain Delano responded; but while doing so, his attention was drawn to nething passing on the deck below: among the crowd climbing the landward warks, anxiously watching the coming boat, two blacks, to all appearances identally incommoded by one of the sailors, flew out against him with rible curses, which the sailor someway resenting, the two blacks dashed him he deck and jumped upon him, despite the earnest cries of the oakum-kers.

Don Benito," said Captain Delano quickly, "do you see what is going on re? Look!"

But, seized by his cough, the Spaniard staggered, with both hands to his face, the point of falling. Captain Delano would have supported him, but the vant was more alert, who, with one hand sustaining his master, with the er applied the cordial. Don Benito, restored, the black withdrew his support, ping aside a little, but dutifully remaining within call of a whisper. Such cretion was here evinced as quite wiped away, in the visitor's eyes, any mish of impropriety which might have attached to the attendant, from the ecorous conferences before mentioned; showing, too, that if the servant re to blame, it might be more the master's fault than his own, since when left iimself he could conduct thus well.

His glance thus called away from the spectacle of disorder to the more asing one before him, Captain Delano could not avoid again congratulating 1 Benito upon possessing such a servant, who, though perhaps a little too ward now and then, must upon the whole be invaluable to one in the alid's situation.

Tell me, Don Benito," he added, with a smile- "I should like to have your man e myself- what will you take for him? Would fifty doubloons be any object?"

Master wouldn't part with Babo for a thousand doubloons," murmured the ck, overhearing the offer, and taking it in earnest, and, with the strange ity of a faithful slave appreciated by his master, scorning to hear so paltry a uation put upon him by a stranger. But Don Benito, apparently hardly yet npletely restored, and again interrupted by his cough, made but some ken reply.

Soon his physical distress became so great, affecting his mind, tool)arently, that, as if to screen the sad spectacle, the servant gently conducted master below.

Left to himself, the American, to while away the time till his boat should ive, would have pleasantly accosted some one of the few Spanish seamen he v; but recalling something that Don Benito had said touching their ill duct, he refrained, as a shipmaster indisposed to countenance cowardice or aithfulness in seamen.

25

While, with these thoughts, standing with eye directed forward toward the handful of sailors- suddenly he thought that some of them returned the glance and with a sort of meaning. He rubbed his eyes, and looked again; but again seemed to see the same thing. Under a new form, but more obscure than any previous one, the old suspicions recurred, but, in the absence of Don Benito, with less of panic than before. Despite the bad account given of the sailors, Captain Delano resolved forthwith to accost one of them. Descending the poop he made his way through the blacks, his movement drawing a queer cry from the oakum-pickers, prompted by whom the Negroes, twitching each other aside, divided before him; but, as if curious to see what was the object of this deliberate visit to their Ghetto, closing in behind, in tolerable order, followed the white stranger up. His progress thus proclaimed as by mounted kings-at-arms, and escorted as by a Caffre guard of honour, Captain Delano, assuming good-humoured, off-hand air, continued to advance; now and then saying a blithe word to the Negroes, and his eye curiously surveying the white faces, here and there sparsely mixed in with the blacks, like stray white pawns venturously involved in the ranks of the chessmen opposed.

While thinking which of them to select for his purpose, he chanced to observe a sailor seated on the deck engaged in tarring the strap of a large block, with a circle of blacks squatted round him inquisitively eyeing the process.

The mean employment of the man was in contrast with something superior in his figure. His hand, black with continually thrusting it into the tar-pot held for him by a Negro, seemed not naturally allied to his face, a face which would have been a very fine one but for its haggardness. Whether this haggardness had aught to do with criminality could not be determined; since, as intense heat and cold, though unlike, produce like sensations, so innocence and guilt, when through casual association with mental pain, stamping any visible impress, use one seal- a hacked one.

Not again that this reflection occurred to Captain Delano at the time, charitable man as he was. Rather another idea. Because observing so singular haggardness to be combined with a dark eye, averted as in trouble and shame and then, however illogically, uniting in his mind his own private suspicions of the crew with the confessed ill-opinion on the part of their captain, he was insensibly operated upon by certain general notions, which, while disconnecting pain and abashment from virtue, as invariably link them with vice.

If, indeed, there be any wickedness on board this ship, thought Captain Delano, be sure that man there has fouled his hand in it, even as now he fouls it in the pitch. I don't like to accost him. I will speak to this other, this old Jack here on the windlass.

He advanced to an old Barcelona tar, in ragged red breeches and dirty night-
), cheeks trenched and bronzed, whiskers dense as thorn hedges. Seated
ween two sleepy-looking Africans, this mariner, like his younger shipmate,
s employed upon some rigging- splicing a cable- the sleepy-looking blacks
forming the inferior function of holding the outer parts of the ropes for him.

Jpon Captain Delano's approach, the man at once hung his head below its
vious level; the one necessary for business. It appeared as if he desired to be
ught absorbed, with more than common fidelity, in his task. Being
dressed, he glanced up, but with what seemed a furtive, diffident air, which
strangely enough on his weather-beaten visage, much as if a grizzly bear,
tead of growling and biting, should simper and cast sheep's eyes. He was
ced several questions concerning the voyage- questions purposely referring
several particulars in Don Benito's narrative- not previously corroborated by
se impulsive cries greeting the visitor on first coming on board. The
estions were briefly answered, confirming all that remained to be confirmed
he story. The Negroes about the windlass joined in with the old sailor, but,
they became talkative, he by degrees became mute, and at length quite glum,
med morosely unwilling to answer more questions, and yet, all the while,
s ursine air was somehow mixed with his sheepish one.

Despairing of getting into unembarrassed talk with such a centaur, Captain
lano, after glancing round for a more promising countenance, but seeing
ne, spoke pleasantly to the blacks to make way for him; and so, amid various
ns and grimaces, returned to the poop, feeling a little strange at first, he
ild hardly tell why, but upon the whole with regained confidence in Benito
eno.

How plainly, thought he, did that old whiskerando yonder betray a
nsciousness of ill-desert. No doubt, when he saw me coming, he dreaded lest
pprised by his captain of the crew's general misbehaviour, came with sharp
rds for him, and so down with his head. And yet- and yet, now that I think of
hat very old fellow, if I err not, was one of those who seemed so earnestly
ing me here awhile since. Ah, these currents spin one's head round almost
much as they do the ship. Ha, there now's a pleasant sort of sunny sight;
te sociable, too.

His attention had been drawn to a slumbering Negress, partly disclosed
ough the lace-work of some rigging, lying, with youthful limbs carelessly
posed, under the lee of the bulwarks, like a doe in the shade of a woodland
k. Sprawling at her lapped breasts was her wide-awake fawn, stark naked,
black little body half lifted from the deck, crosswise with its dam's; its hands,
two paws, clambering upon her; its mouth and nose ineffectually rooting to
at the mark; and meantime giving a vexatious half-grunt, blending with the
nposed snore of the Negress.

The uncommon vigour of the child at length roused the mother. She started up, at distance facing Captain Delano. But, as if not at all concerned at the attitude in which she had been caught, delightedly she caught the child up, with maternal transports, covering it with kisses.

There's naked nature, now; pure tenderness and love, thought Captain Delano, well pleased.

This incident prompted him to remark the other Negresses more particularly than before. He was gratified with their manners; like most uncivilized women they seemed at once tender of heart and tough of constitution; equally ready to die for their infants or fight for them. Unsophisticated as leopardesses; loving as doves. Ah! thought Captain Delano, these perhaps are some of the very women whom Mungo Park saw in Africa, and gave such a noble account of.

These natural sights somehow insensibly deepened his confidence and ease. At last he looked to see how his boat was getting on; but it was still pretty remote. He turned to see if Don Benito had returned; but he had not.

To change the scene, as well as to please himself with a leisurely observation of the coming boat, stepping over into the mizzen-chains he clambered his way into the starboard quarter-galley; one of those abandoned Venetian-looking water-balconies previously mentioned; retreats cut off from the deck. As his foot pressed the half-damp, half-dry sea-mosses matting the place, and a chance phantom cat's-paw- an islet of breeze, unheralded, unfollowed- as this ghostly cat's-paw came fanning his cheek, his glance fell upon the row of small, round dead-lights, all closed like coppered eyes of the coffined, and the state-cabin door, once connecting with the gallery, even as the dead-lights had once looked out upon it, but now caulked fast like a sarcophagus lid, to a purple-black, tarred-over panel, threshold, and post; and he bethought him of the time, when that state-cabin and this state-balcony had heard the voices of the Spanish king's officers, and the forms of the Lima viceroy's daughters had perhaps leaned where he stood- as these and other images flitted through his mind, as the cat's-paw through the calm, gradually he felt rising a dreamy inquietude, like that of one who alone on the prairie feels unrest from the repose of the noon.

He leaned against the carved balustrade, again looking off toward his boat; but found his eye falling upon the ribboned grass, trailing along the ship's water-line, straight as a border of green box; and parterres of sea-weed, broad ovals and crescents, floating nigh and far, with what seemed long formal alleys between, crossing the terraces of swells, and sweeping round as if leading to the grottoes below. And overhanging all was the balustrade by his arm, which, partly stained with pitch and partly embossed with moss, seemed the charred ruin of some summer-house in a grand garden long running to waste.

Trying to break one charm, he was but becharmed anew. Though upon the le sea, he seemed in some far inland country; prisoner in some deserted teau, left to stare at empty grounds, and peer out at vague roads, where er wagon or wayfarer passed.

But these enchantments were a little disenchanted as his eye fell on the roded main-chains. Of an ancient style, massy and rusty in link, shackle and t, they seemed even more fit for the ship's present business than the one for ich probably she had been built.

Presently he thought something moved nigh the chains. He rubbed his eyes, l looked hard. Groves of rigging were about the chains; and there, peering m behind a great stay, like an Indian from behind a hemlock, a Spanish lor, a marlingspike in his hand, was seen, who made what seemed an perfect gesture toward the balcony- but immediately, as if alarmed by some ancing step along the deck within, vanished into the recesses of the hempen est, like a poacher.

What meant this? Something the man had sought to communicate, peknown to any one, even to his captain? Did the secret involve aught favourable to his captain? Were those previous misgivings of Captain ano's about to be verified? Or, in his haunted mood at the moment, had ne random, unintentional motion of the man, while busy with the stay, as if airing it, been mistaken for a significant beckoning?

Not unbewildered, again he gazed off for his boat. But it was temporarily den by a rocky spur of the isle. As with some eagerness he bent forward, tching for the first shooting view of its beak, the balustrade gave way before like charcoal. Had he not clutched an outreaching rope he would have en into the sea. The crash, though feeble, and the fall, though hollow, of the ten fragments, must have been overheard. He glanced up. With sober iosity peering down upon him was one of the old oakum-pickers, slipped m his perch to an outside boom; while below the old Negro- and, invisible to , reconnoitring from a port-hole like a fox from the mouth of its den- uched the Spanish sailor again. From something suddenly suggested by the n's air, the mad idea now darted into Captain Delano's mind: that Don lito's plea of indisposition, in withdrawing below, was but a pretence: that was engaged there maturing some plot, of which the sailor, by some means ning an inkling, had a mind to warn the stranger against; incited, it may be, gratitude for a kind word on first boarding the ship. Was it from foreseeing ne possible interference like this, that Don Benito had, beforehand, given h a bad character of his sailors, while praising the Negroes; though, indeed, former seemed as docile as the latter the contrary? The whites, too, by ure, were the shrewder race. A man with some evil design, would not he be ly to speak well of that stupidity which was blind to his depravity, and malign that intelligence from which it might not be hidden? Not unlikely, perhaps. But if the whites had dark secrets concerning Don Benito, could then Don Benito be any way in complicity with the blacks? But they were too stupi Besides, who ever heard of a white so far a renegade as to apostatize from his very species almost, by leaguing in against it with Negroes? These difficulties recalled former ones. Lost in their mazes, Captain Delano, who had now regained the deck, was uneasily advancing along it, when he observed a new face: an aged sailor seated cross-legged near the main hatchway. His skin was shrunk up with wrinkles like a pelican's empty pouch; his hair frosted; his countenance grave and composed. His hands were full of ropes, which he was working into a large knot. Some blacks were about him obligingly dipping the strands for him, here and there, as the exigencies of the operation demanded

Captain Delano crossed over to him, and stood in silence surveying the kno his mind, by a not uncongenial transition, passing from its own entanglement to those of the hemp. For intricacy such a knot he had never seen in an American ship, or indeed any other. The old man looked like an Egyptian prie making Gordian knots for the temple of Ammon. The knot seemed a combination of double-bowline-knot, treble-crown-knot, back-handed-well-knot, knot-in-and-out-knot, and jamming-knot.

At last, puzzled to comprehend the meaning of such a knot, Captain Delanc addressed the knotter:-

"What are you knotting there, my man?"

"The knot," was the brief reply, without looking up.

"So it seems; but what is it for?"

"For some one else to undo," muttered back the old man, plying his fingers harder than ever, the knot being now nearly completed.

While Captain Delano stood watching him, suddenly the old man threw the knot toward him, and said in broken English,- the first heard in the ship,- something to this effect- "Undo it, cut it, quick." It was said lowly, but with su condensation of rapidity, that the long, slow words in Spanish, which had preceded and followed, almost operated as covers to the brief English betwee

For a moment, knot in hand, and knot in head, Captain Delano stood mute; while, without further heeding him, the old man was now intent upon other ropes. Presently there was a slight stir behind Captain Delano. Turning, he sa the chained Negro, Atufal, standing quietly there. The next moment the old sailor rose, muttering, and, followed by his subordinate Negroes, removed to the forward part of the ship, where in the crowd he disappeared.

An elderly Negro, in a clout like an infant's, and with a pepper and salt hea and a kind of attorney air, now approached Captain Delano. In tolerable

30

nish, and with a good-natured, knowing wink, he informed him that the old
tter was simple-witted, but harmless; often playing his old tricks. The Negro
cluded by begging the knot, for of course the stranger would not care to be
ubled with it. Unconsciously, it was handed to him. With a sort of conge, the
gro received it, and turning his back ferreted into it like a detective Custom
se officer after smuggled laces. Soon, with some African word, equivalent to
aw, he tossed the knot overboard.

All this is very queer now, thought Captain Delano, with a qualmish sort of
otion; but as one feeling incipient seasickness, he strove, by ignoring the
mptoms, to get rid of the malady. Once more he looked off for his boat. To his
ight, it was now again in view, leaving the rocky spur astern.

he sensation here experienced, after at first relieving his uneasiness, with
oreseen efficiency, soon began to remove it. The less distant sight of that
ll-known boat- showing it, not as before, half blended with the haze, but with
line defined, so that its individuality, like a man's, was manifest; that boat,
ver by name, which, though now in strange seas, had often pressed the beach
Captain Delano's home, and, brought to its threshold for repairs, had
iliarly lain there, as a Newfoundland dog; the sight of that household boat
ked a thousand trustful associations, which, contrasted with previous
picions, filled Him not only with lightsome confidence, but somehow with
f humorous self-reproaches at his former lack of it.

What, I, Amasa Delano- Jack of the Beach, as they called me when a lad- I,
asa; the same that, duck-satchel in hand, used to paddle along the waterside
he schoolhouse made from the old hulk;- I, little Jack of the Beach, that used
o berrying with cousin Nat and the rest; I to be murdered here at the ends of
 earth, on board a haunted pirate-ship by a horrible Spaniard?- Too
sensical to think of! Who would murder Amasa Delano? His conscience is
an. There is some one above. Fie, fie, Jack of the Beach! you are a child
eed; a child of the second childhood, old boy; you are beginning to dote and
ol, I'm afraid."

ight of heart and foot, he stepped aft, and there was met by Don Benito's
vant, who, with a pleasing expression, responsive to his own present
lings, informed him that his master had recovered from the effects of his
ghing fit, and had just ordered him to go present his compliments to his
d guest, Don Amasa, and say that he (Don Benito) would soon have the
piness to rejoin him.

here now, do you mark that? again thought Captain Delano, walking the
p. What a donkey I was. This kind gentleman who here sends me his kind
mpliments, he, but ten minutes ago, dark-lantern in hand, was dodging round
ne old grind-stone in the hold, sharpening a hatchet for me, I thought. Well,
ll; these long calms have a morbid effect on the mind, I've often heard,

though I never believed it before. Ha! glancing toward the boat; there's Rover good dog; a white bone in her mouth. A pretty big bone though, seems to me. What? Yes, she has fallen afoul of the bubbling tide-rip there. It sets her the other way, too, for the time. Patience.

It was now about noon, though, from the greyness of everything, it seemed be getting toward dusk.

The calm was confirmed. In the far distance, away from the influence of la the leaden ocean seemed laid out and leaded up, its course finished, soul gon defunct. But the current from landward, where the ship was, increased; silen sweeping her further and further toward the tranced waters beyond.

Still, from his knowledge of those latitudes, cherishing hopes of a breeze, a a fair and fresh one, at any moment, Captain Delano, despite present prospec buoyantly counted upon bringing the San Dominick safely to anchor ere nigh The distance swept over was nothing; since, with a good wind, ten minutes' sailing would retrace more than sixty minutes' drifting. Meantime, one mome turning to mark Rover fighting the tide-rip, and the next to see Don Benito approaching, he continued walking the poop.

Gradually he felt a vexation arising from the delay of his boat; this soon merged into uneasiness; and at last, his eye falling continually, as from a stag box into the pit, upon the strange crowd before and below him, and by-and-b recognizing there the face- now composed to indifference- of the Spanish sail who had seemed to beckon from the main-chains, something of his old trepidations returned.

Ah, thought he- gravely enough- this is like the ague: because it went off, it follows not that it won't come back.

Though ashamed of the relapse, he could not altogether subdue it; and so, exerting his good nature to the utmost, insensibly he came to a compromise.

Yes, this is a strange craft; a strange history, too, and strange folks on boar But- nothing more.

By way of keeping his mind out of mischief till the boat should arrive, he tried to occupy it with turning over and over, in a purely speculative sort of way, some lesser peculiarities of the captain and crew. Among others, four curious points recurred.

First, the affair of the Spanish lad assailed with a knife by the slave boy; an act winked at by Don Benito. Second, the tyranny in Don Benito's treatment c Atufal, the black; as if a child should lead a bull of the Nile by the ring in his nose. Third, the trampling of the sailor by the two Negroes; a piece of insolen passed over without so much as a reprimand. Fourth, the cringing submissio their master of all the ship's underlings, mostly blacks; as if by the least advertence they feared to draw down his despotic displeasure.

Coupling these points, they seemed somewhat contradictory. But what then, thought Captain Delano, glancing toward his now nearing boat,- what then? Why, this Don Benito is a very capricious commander. But he is not the first of the sort I have seen; though it's true he rather exceeds any other. But as a nation- continued he in his reveries- these Spaniards are all an odd set; the very word Spaniard has a curious, conspirator, Guy-Fawkish twang to it. And yet, I dare say, Spaniards in the main are as good folks as any in Duxbury, Massachusetts. Ah, good! At last Rover has come.

As, with its welcome freight, the boat touched the side, the oakum-pickers, with venerable gestures, sought to restrain the blacks, who, at the sight of three gurried water-casks in its bottom, and a pile of wilted pumpkins in its bow, leaning over the bulwarks in disorderly raptures.

Don Benito with his servant now appeared; his coming, perhaps, hastened by hearing the noise. Of him Captain Delano sought permission to serve out the water, so that all might share alike, and none injure themselves by unfair access. But sensible, and, on Don Benito's account, kind as this offer was, it was received with what seemed impatience; as if aware that he lacked energy as a commander, Don Benito, with the true jealousy of weakness, resented as an affront any interference. So, at least, Captain Delano inferred.

In another moment the casks were being hoisted in, when some of the eager negroes accidentally jostled Captain Delano, where he stood by the gangway; so that, unmindful of Don Benito, yielding to the impulse of the moment, with good-natured authority he bade the blacks stand back; to enforce his words making use of a half-mirthful, half-menacing gesture. Instantly the blacks paused, just where they were, each Negro and Negress suspended in his or her posture, exactly as the word had found them- for a few seconds continuing so- while, as between the responsive posts of a telegraph, an unknown syllable ran from man to man among the perched oakum-pickers. While Captain Delano's attention was fixed by this scene, suddenly the hatchet-polishers half rose, and a rapid cry came from Don Benito.

Thinking that at the signal of the Spaniard he was about to be massacred, Captain Delano would have sprung for his boat, but paused, as the oakum-pickers, dropping down into the crowd with earnest exclamations, forced every white and every Negro back, at the same moment, with gestures friendly and familiar, almost jocose, bidding him, in substance, not be a fool. Simultaneously the hatchet-polishers resumed their seats, quietly as so many tailors, and at once, as if nothing had happened, the work of hoisting in the casks was resumed, whites and blacks singing at the tackle.

Captain Delano glanced toward Don Benito. As he saw his meagre form in the act of recovering itself from reclining in the servant's arms, into which the agitated invalid had fallen, he could not but marvel at the panic by which himself had been surprised on the darting supposition that such a commander who upon a legitimate occasion, so trivial, too, as it now appeared, could lose self-command, was, with energetic iniquity, going to bring about his murder.

The casks being on deck, Captain Delano was handed a number of jars and cups by one of the steward's aides, who, in the name of Don Benito, entreated him to do as he had proposed: dole out the water. He complied, with republic impartiality as to this republican element, which always seeks one level, serv the oldest white no better than the youngest black; excepting, indeed, poor D Benito, whose condition, if not rank, demanded an extra allowance. To him, in the first place, Captain Delano presented a fair pitcher of the fluid; but, thirsti as he was for fresh water, Don Benito quaffed not a drop until after several grave bows and salutes: a reciprocation of courtesies which the sight-loving Africans hailed with clapping of hands.

Two of the less wilted pumpkins being reserved for the cabin table, the residue were minced up on the spot for the general regalement. But the soft bread, sugar, and bottled cider, Captain Delano would have given the Spaniar alone, and in chief Don Benito; but the latter objected; which disinterestedne: on his part, not a little pleased the American; and so mouthfuls all around wen given alike to whites and blacks; excepting one bottle of cider, which Babo insisted upon setting aside for his master.

Here it may be observed that as, on the first visit of the boat, the American had not permitted his men to board the ship, neither did he now; being unwilling to add to the confusion of the decks.

Not uninfluenced by the peculiar good humour at present prevailing, and f the time oblivious of any but benevolent thoughts, Captain Delano, who from recent indications counted upon a breeze within an hour or two at furthest, despatched the boat back to the sealer with orders for all the hands that could be spared immediately to set about rafting casks to the watering-place and filling them. Likewise he bade word be carried to his chief officer, that if again present expectation the ship was not brought to anchor by sunset, he need be under no concern, for as there was to be a full moon that night, he (Captain Delano) would remain on board ready to play the pilot, should the wind come soon or late.

As the two captains stood together, observing the departing boat- the serva as it happened having just spied a spot on his master's velvet sleeve, and silently engaged rubbing it out- the American expressed his regrets that the S Dominick had no boats; none, at least, but the unseaworthy old hulk of the lon boat, which, warped as a camel's skeleton in the desert, and almost as bleache

34

pot-wise inverted amidships, one side a little tipped, furnishing a
terraneous sort of den for family groups of the blacks, mostly women and
all children; who, squatting on old mats below, or perched above in the dark
ne, on the elevated seats, were descried, some distance within, like a social
:le of bats, sheltering in some friendly cave; at intervals, ebon flights of
ked boys and girls, three or four years old, darting in and out of the den's
uth.

"Had you three or four boats now, Don Benito," said Captain Delano, "I think
t, by tugging at the oars, your Negroes here might help along matters some.-
l you sail from port without boats, Don Benito?"

"They were stove in the gales, Senor."

"That was bad. Many men, too, you lost then. Boats and men.- Those must
ve been hard gales, Don Benito."

"Past all speech," cringed the Spaniard.

"Tell me, Don Benito," continued his companion with increased interest, "tell
, were these gales immediately off the pitch of Cape Horn?"

"Cape Horn?- who spoke of Cape Horn?"

"Yourself did, when giving me an account of your voyage," answered Captain
ano with almost equal astonishment at this eating of his own words, even as
ever seemed eating his own heart, on the part of the Spaniard. "You yourself,
n Benito, spoke of Cape Horn," he emphatically repeated.

The Spaniard turned, in a sort of stooping posture, pausing an instant, as one
)ut to make a plunging exchange of elements, as from air to water.

At this moment a messenger-boy, a white, hurried by, in the regular
rformance of his function carrying the last expired half-hour forward to the
ecastle, from the cabin time-piece, to have it struck at the ship's large bell.

"Master," said the servant, discontinuing his work on the coat sleeve, and
dressing the rapt Spaniard with a sort of timid apprehensiveness, as one
rged with a duty, the discharge of which, it was foreseen, would prove
some to the very person who had imposed it, and for whose benefit it was
ended, "master told me never mind where he was, or how engaged, always to
nind him, to a minute, when shaving-time comes. Miguel has gone to strike
half-hour after noon. It is now, master. Will master go into the cuddy?"

"Ah- yes," answered the Spaniard, starting, somewhat as from dreams into
.lities; then turning upon Captain Delano, he said that ere long he would
ume the conversation.

35

"Then if master means to talk more to Don Amasa," said the servant, "why not let Don Amasa sit by master in the cuddy, and master can talk, and Don Amasa can listen, whileBabo here lathers and strops."

"Yes," said Captain Delano, not unpleased with this sociable plan, "yes, Don Benito, unless you had rather not, I will go with you."

"Be it so, Senor."

As the three passed aft, the American could not but think it another strang instance of his host's capriciousness, this being shaved with such uncommon punctuality in the middle of the day. But he deemed it more than likely that th servant's anxious fidelity had something to do with the matter; inasmuch as t timely interruption served to rally his master from the mood which had evidently been coming upon him.

The place called the cuddy was a light deck-cabin formed by the poop, a so of attic to the large cabin below. Part of it had formerly been the quarters of t officers; but since their death all the partitionings had been thrown down, an the whole interior converted into one spacious and airy marine hall; for absence of fine furniture and picturesque disarray, of odd appurtenances, somewhat answering to the wide, cluttered hall of some eccentric bachelor squire in the country, who hangs his shooting-jacket and tobacco-pouch on d antlers, and keeps his fishing-rod, tongs, and walking-stick in the same corne

The similitude was heightened, if not originally suggested, by glimpses of t surrounding sea; since, in one aspect, the country and the ocean seem cousin german.

The floor of the cuddy was matted. Overhead, four or five old muskets wer stuck into horizontal holes along the beams. On one side was a claw-footed ol table lashed to the deck; a thumbed missal on it, and over it a small, meagre crucifix attached to the bulkhead. Under the table lay a dented cutlass or two with a hacked harpoon, among some melancholy old rigging, like a heap of pc friar's girdles. There were also two long, sharp-ribbed settees of malacca can black with age, and uncomfortable to look at as inquisitors' racks, with a larg misshapen arm-chair, which, furnished with a rude barber's crutch at the bac working with a screw, seemed some grotesque Middle Age engine of torment flag locker was in one corner, exposing various coloured bunting, some rollec up, others half unrolled, still others tumbled. Opposite was a cumbrous washstand, of black mahogany, all of one block, with a pedestal, like a font, an over it a railed shelf, containing combs, brushes, and other implements of the toilet. A tom hammock of stained grass swung near; the sheets tossed, and th pillow wrinkled up like a brow, as if whoever slept here slept but illy, with alternate visitations of sad thoughts and bad dreams.

'he further extremity of the cuddy, overhanging the ship's stern, was pierced
h three openings, windows or port-holes, according as men or cannon might
r, socially or unsocially, out of them. At present neither men nor cannon
·e seen, though huge ring-bolts and other rusty iron fixtures of the wood-
rk hinted of twenty-four-pounders.

;lancing toward the hammock as he entered, Captain Delano said, "You sleep
e, Don Benito?"

Yes, Senor, since we got into mild weather."

This seems a sort of dormitory, sitting-room, sail-loft, chapel, armoury, and
vate closet together, Don Benito," added Captain Delano, looking around.

Yes, Senor; events have not been favourable to much order in my
angements."

Here the servant, napkin on arm, made a motion as if waiting his master's
·d pleasure. Don Benito signified his readiness, when, seating him in the
lacca arm-chair, and for the guest's convenience drawing opposite it one of
settees, the servant commenced operations by throwing back his master's
lar and loosening his cravat.

There is something in the Negro which, in a peculiar way, fits him for
·cations about one's person. Most Negroes are natural valets and hair-
ssers; taking to the comb and brush congenially as to the castanets, and
irishing them apparently with almost equal satisfaction. There is, too, a
ooth tact about them in this employment, with a marvellous, noiseless,
ling briskness, not ungraceful in its way, singularly pleasing to behold, and
l more so to be the manipulated subject of. And above all is the great gift of
·d humour. Not the mere grin or laugh is here meant. Those were unsuitable.
 a certain easy cheerfulness, harmonious in every glance and gesture; as
ugh God had set the whole Negro to some pleasant tune.

When to all this is added the docility arising from the unaspiring
tentment of a limited mind, and that susceptibility of blind attachment
netimes inhering in indisputable inferiors, one readily perceives why those
ochondriacs, Johnson and Byron- it may be something like the
ochondriac, Benito Cereno- took to their hearts, almost to the exclusion of
 entire white race, their serving men, the Negroes, Barber and Fletcher. But
here be that in the Negro which exempts him from the inflicted sourness of
 morbid or cynical mind, how, in his most prepossessing aspects, must he
bear to a benevolent one? When at ease with respect to exterior things,
otain Delano's nature was not only benign, but familiarly and humorously so.
nome, he had often taken rare satisfaction in sitting in his door, watching
ne free man of colour at his work or play. If on a voyage he chanced to have a
ck sailor, invariably he was on chatty, and half-gamesome terms with him. In

fact, like most men of a good, blithe heart, Captain Delano took to Negroes, n॓ philanthropically, but genially, just as other men to Newfoundland dogs.

Hitherto the circumstances in which he found the San Dominick had repressed the tendency. But in the cuddy, relieved from his former uneasines॓ and, for various reasons, more sociably inclined than at any previous period ॔ the day, and seeing the coloured servant, napkin on arm, so debonair about h master, in a business so familiar as that of shaving, too, all his old weakness f॓ Negroes returned.

Among other things, he was amused with an odd instance of the African lo of bright colours and fine shows, in the black's informally taking from the fla॓ locker a great piece of bunting of all hues, and lavishly tucking it under his master's chin for an apron.

The mode of shaving among the Spaniards is a little different from what it with other nations. They have a basin, specially called a barber's basin, which on one side is scooped out, so as accurately to receive the chin, against which is closely held in lathering; which is done, not with a brush, but with soap dipped in the water of the basin and rubbed on the face.

In the present instance salt-water was used for lack of better; and the part lathered were only the upper lip, and low down under the throat, all the rest being cultivated beard.

These preliminaries being somewhat novel to Captain Delano he sat curiously eyeing them, so that no conversation took place, nor for the presen॓ did Don Benito appear disposed to renew any.

Setting down his basin, the Negro searched among the razors, as for the sharpest, and having found it, gave it an additional edge by expertly stroppin॓ on the firm, smooth, oily skin of his open palm; he then made a gesture as if t begin, but midway stood suspended for an instant, one hand elevating the razor, the other professionally dabbling among the bubbling suds on the Spaniard's lank neck. Not unaffected by the close sight of the gleaming steel, Don Benito nervously shuddered, his usual ghastliness was heightened by th lather, which lather, again, was intensified in its hue by the sootiness of the Negro's body. Altogether the scene was somewhat peculiar, at least to Captai Delano, nor, as he saw the two thus postured, could he resist the vagary, that the black he saw a headsman, and in the white, a man at the block. But this w one of those antic conceits, appearing and vanishing in a breath, from which, perhaps, the best regulated mind is not free.

Meantime the agitation of the Spaniard had a little loosened the bunting fr॓ around him, so that one broad fold swept curtain-like over the chair-arm to t॓ floor, revealing, amid a profusion of armorial bars and ground-colours- black

e and yellow- a closed castle in a blood-red field diagonal with a lion
npant in a white.

"The castle and the lion," exclaimed Captain Delano- "why, Don Benito, this is
 flag of Spain you use here. It's well it's only I, and not the King, that sees
s," he added with a smile, "but"- turning toward the black,- "it's all one, I
)pose, so the colours be gay," which playful remark did not fail somewhat to
<le the Negro.

"Now, master," he said, readjusting the flag, and pressing the head gently
ther back into the crotch of the chair; "now master," and the steel glanced
h the throat.

Again Don Benito faintly shuddered.

"You must not shake so, master.- See, Don Amasa, master always shakes
en I shave him. And yet master knows I never yet have drawn blood, though
 true, if master will shake so, I may some of these times. Now, master," he
itinued. "And now, Don Amasa, please go on with your talk about the gale,
1 all that, master can hear, and between times master can answer."

"Ah yes, these gales," said Captain Delano; "but the more I think of your
/age, Don Benito, the more I wonder, not at the gales, terrible as they must
/e been, but at the disastrous interval following them. For here, by your
·ount, have you been these two months and more getting from Cape Horn to
Maria, a distance which I myself, with a good wind, have sailed in a few days.
ie, you had calms, and long ones, but to be becalmed for two months, that is,
east, unusual. Why, Don Benito, had almost any other gentleman told me
:h a story, I should have been half disposed to a little incredulity."

Here an involuntary expression came over the Spaniard, similar to that just
·ore on the deck, and whether it was the start he gave, or a sudden gawky roll
·he hull in the calm, or a momentary unsteadiness of the servant's hand;
·wever it was, just then the razor drew blood, spots of which stained the
 amy lather under the throat; immediately the black barber drew back his
·el, and remaining in his professional attitude, back to Captain Delano, and
·e to Don Benito, held up the trickling razor, saying, with a sort of half
norous sorrow, "See, master,- you shook so- here's Babo's first blood."

No sword drawn before James the First of England, no assassination in that
iid King's presence, could have produced a more terrified aspect than was
w presented by Don Benito.

Poor fellow, thought Captain Delano, so nervous he can't even bear the sight
barber's blood; and this unstrung, sick man, is it credible that I should have
agined he meant to spill all my blood, who can't endure the sight of one little
)p of his own? Surely, Amasa Delano, you have been beside yourself this day.
ll it not when you get home, sappy Amasa. Well, well, he looks like a

39

murderer, doesn't he? More like as if himself were to be done for. Well, well, this day's experience shall be a good lesson.

Meantime, while these things were running through the honest seaman's mind, the servant had taken the napkin from his arm, and to Don Benito had said: "But answer Don Amasa, please, master, while I wipe this ugly stuff off t razor, and strop it again."

As he said the words, his face was turned half round, so as to be alike visibl to the Spaniard and the American, and seemed by its expression to hint, that I was desirous, by getting his master to go on with the conversation, considerately to withdraw his attention from the recent annoying accident. A glad to snatch the offered relief, Don Benito resumed, rehearsing to Captain Delano, that not only were the calms of unusual duration, but the ship had fallen in with obstinate currents and other things he added, some of which w but repetitions of former statements, to explain how it came to pass that the passage from Cape Horn to St. Maria had been so exceedingly long, now and then mingling with his words, incidental praises, less qualified than before, to the blacks, for their general good conduct.

These particulars were not given consecutively, the servant now and then using his razor, and so, between the intervals of shaving, the story and panegyric went on with more than usual huskiness.

To Captain Delano's imagination, now again not wholly at rest, there was something so hollow in the Spaniard's manner, with apparently some reciprocal hollowness in the servant's dusky comment of silence, that the ide, flashed across him, that possibly master and man, for some unknown purpos were acting out, both in word and deed, nay, to the very tremor of Don Benito limbs, some juggling play before him. Neither did the suspicion of collusion la apparent support, from the fact of those whispered conferences before mentioned. But then, what could be the object of enacting this play of the barber before him? At last, regarding the notion as a whimsy, insensibly suggested, perhaps, by the theatrical aspect of Don Benito in his harlequin ensign, Captain Delano speedily banished it.

The shaving over, the servant bestirred himself with a small bottle of scent waters, pouring a few drops on the head, and then diligently rubbing; the vehemence of the exercise causing the muscles of his face to twitch rather strangely.

His next operation was with comb, scissors and brush; going round and round, smoothing a curl here, clipping an unruly whisker-hair there, giving a graceful sweep to the temple-lock, with other impromptu touches evincing th hand of a master; while, like any resigned gentleman in barber's hands, Don Benito bore all, much less uneasily, at least, than he had done the razoring;

eed, he sat so pale and rigid now, that the Negro seemed a Nubian sculptor
shing off a white statue-head.

All being over at last, the standard of Spain removed, tumbled up, and tossed
k into the flag-locker, the Negro's warm breath blowing away any stray hair
ich might have lodged down his master's neck; collar and cravat readjusted;
peck of lint whisked off the velvet lapel; all this being done; backing off a
le space, and pausing with an expression of subdued self-complacency, the
vant for a moment surveyed his master, as, in toilet at least, the creature of
own tasteful hands.

Captain Delano playfully complimented him upon his achievement; at the
ne time congratulating Don Benito.

But neither sweet waters, nor shampooing, nor fidelity, nor sociality,
ighted the Spaniard. Seeing him relapsing into forbidding gloom, and still
naining seated, Captain Delano, thinking that his presence was undesired
t then, withdrew, on pretence of seeing whether, as he had prophesied, any
ns of a breeze were visible.

Walking forward to the mainmast, he stood awhile thinking over the scene,
I not without some undefined misgivings, when he heard a noise near the
ldy, and turning, saw the Negro, his hand to his cheek. Advancing, Captain
ano perceived that the cheek was bleeding. He was about to ask the cause,
en the Negro's wailing soliloquy enlightened him.

'Ah, when will master get better from his sickness; only the sour heart that
ir sickness breeds made him serve Babo so; cutting Babo with the razor,
:ause, only by accident, Babo had given master one little scratch; and for the
't time in so many a day, too. Ah, ah, ah," holding his hand to his face.

s it possible, thought Captain Delano; was it to wreak in private his Spanish
te against this poor friend of his, that Don Benito, by his sullen manner,
pelled me to withdraw? Ah, this slavery breeds ugly passions in man! Poor
ow!

He was about to speak in sympathy to the Negro, but with a timid reluctance
now re-entered the cuddy.

Presently master and man came forth; Don Benito leaning on his servant as if
thing had happened.

But a sort of love-quarrel, after all, thought Captain Delano.

He accosted Don Benito, and they slowly walked together. They had gone but
:w paces, when the steward-a tall, rajah-looking mulatto, orientally set off
h a pagoda turban formed by three or four Madras handkerchiefs wound
put his head, tier on tier- approaching with a salaam, announced lunch in the
in.

41

On their way thither, the two captains were preceded by the mulatto, who, turning round as he advanced, with continual smiles and bows, ushered them in, a display of elegance which quite completed the insignificance of the small bare-headed Babo, who, as if not unconscious of inferiority, eyed askance the graceful steward. But in part, Captain Delano imputed his jealous watchfulne to that peculiar feeling which the full-blooded African entertains for the adulterated one. As for the steward, his manner, if not bespeaking much dign of self-respect, yet evidenced his extreme desire to please; which is doubly meritorious, as at once Christian and Chesterfieldian.

Captain Delano observed with interest that while the complexion of the mulatto was hybrid, his physiognomy was European; classically so.

"Don Benito," whispered he, "I am glad to see this usher-of-the-golden-rod yours; the sight refutes an ugly remark once made to me by a Barbados plant that when a mulatto has a regular European face, look out for him; he is a de But see, your steward here has features more regular than King George's of England; and yet there he nods, and bows, and smiles; a king, indeed- the kin of kind hearts and polite fellows. What a pleasant voice he has, too?"

"He has, Senor."

"But, tell me, has he not, so far as you have known him, always proved a good, worthy fellow?" said Captain Delano, pausing, while with a final genuflexion the steward disappeared into the cabin; "come, for the reason ju: mentioned, I am curious to know."

"Francesco is a good man," rather sluggishly responded Don Benito, like a phlegmatic appreciator, who would neither find fault nor flatter.

"Ah, I thought so. For it were strange indeed, and not very creditable to us white-skins, if a little of our blood mixed with the African's, should, far from improving the latter's quality, have the sad effect of pouring vitriolic acid into black broth; improving the hue, perhaps, but not the wholesomeness."

"Doubtless, doubtless, Senor, but"- glancing at Babo- "not to speak of Negroes, your planter's remark I have heard applied to the Spanish and India intermixtures in our provinces. But I know nothing about the matter," he listlessly added.

And here they entered the cabin.

The lunch was a frugal one. Some of Captain Delano's fresh fish and pumpkins, biscuit and salt beef, the reserved bottle of cider, and the San Dominick's last bottle of Canary.

As they entered, Francesco, with two or three coloured aides, was hoverin; over the table giving the last adjustments. Upon perceiving their master they withdrew, Francesco making a smiling conge, and the Spaniard, without

42

descending to notice it, fastidiously remarking to his companion that he
shed not superfluous attendance.

Without companions, host and guest sat down, like a childless married
ple, at opposite ends of the table, Don Benito waving Captain Delano to his
ce, and, weak as he was, insisting upon that gentleman being seated before
iself.

The Negro placed a rug under Don Benito's feet, and a cushion behind his
k, and then stood behind, not his master's chair, but Captain Delano's. At
t, this a little surprised the latter. But it was soon evident that, in taking his
sition, the black was still true to his master; since by facing him he could the
re readily anticipate his slightest want.

This is an uncommonly intelligent fellow of yours, Don Benito," whispered
otain Delano across the table.

You say true, Senor."

During the repast, the guest again reverted to parts of Don Benito's story,
ging further particulars here and there. He inquired how it was that the
rvy and fever should have committed such wholesale havoc upon the
ites, while destroying less than half of the blacks. As if this question
roduced the whole scene of plague before the Spaniard's eyes, miserably
inding him of his solitude in a cabin where before he had had so many
nds and officers round him, his hand shook, his face became hueless, broken
rds escaped; but directly the sane memory of the past seemed replaced by
ane terrors of the present. With starting eyes he stared before him at
ancy. For nothing was to be seen but the hand of his servant pushing the
ary over towards him. At length a few sips served partially to restore him.
made random reference to the different constitutions of races, enabling one
offer more resistance to certain maladies than another. The thought was new
is companion.

Presently Captain Delano, intending to say something to his host concerning
pecuniary part of the business he had undertaken for him, especially- since
was strictly accountable to his owners- with reference to the new suit of
s, and other things of that sort; and naturally preferring to conduct such
irs in private, was desirous that the servant should withdraw; imagining
t Don Benito for a few minutes could dispense with his attendance. He,
vever, waited awhile; thinking that, as the conversation proceeded, Don
ito, without being prompted, would perceive the propriety of the step.

But it was otherwise. At last catching his host's eye, Captain Delano, with a
ht backward gesture of his thumb, whispered, "Don Benito, pardon me, but
re is an interference with the full expression of what I have to say to you."

43

Upon this the Spaniard changed countenance; which was imputed to his resenting the hint, as in some way a reflection upon his servant. After a moment's pause, he assured his guest that the black's remaining with them could be of no disservice; because since losing his officers he had made Babo (whose original office, it now appeared, had been captain of the slaves) not o his constant attendant and companion, but in all things his confidant.

After this, nothing more could be said; though, indeed, Captain Delano cou hardly avoid some little tinge of irritation upon being left ungratified in so inconsiderable a wish, by one, too, for whom he intended such solid services. But it is only his querulousness, thought he; and so filling his glass he proceeded to business.

The price of the sails and other matters was fixed upon. But while this was being done, the American observed that, though his original offer of assistanc had been hailed with hectic animation, yet now when it was reduced to a business transaction, indifference and apathy were betrayed. Don Benito, in fact, appeared to submit to hearing the details more out of regard to commor propriety, than from any impression that weighty benefit to himself and his voyage was involved.

Soon, his manner became still more reserved. The effort was vain to seek t draw him into social talk. Gnawed by his splenetic mood, he sat twitching his beard, while to little purpose the hand of his servant, mute as that on the wal slowly pushed over the Canary.

Lunch being over, they sat down on the cushioned transom; the servant placing a pillow behind his master. The long continuance of the calm had nov affected the atmosphere. Don Benito sighed heavily, as if for breath.

"Why not adjourn to the cuddy," said Captain Delano; "there is more air there." But the host sat silent and motionless.

Meantime his servant knelt before him, with a large fan of feathers. And Francesco, coming in on tiptoes, handed the Negro a little cup of aromatic waters, with which at intervals he chafed his master's brow, smoothing the h along the temples as a nurse does a child's. He spoke no word. He only rested his eye on his master's, as if, amid all Don Benito's distress, a little to refresh spirit by the silent sight of fidelity.

Presently the ship's bell sounded two o'clock; and through the cabin-windows a slight rippling of the sea was discerned; and from the desired direction.

"There," exclaimed Captain Delano, "I told you so, Don Benito, look!"

He had risen to his feet, speaking in a very animated tone, with a view the more to rouse his companion. But though the crimson curtain of the stern-

dow near him that moment fluttered against his pale cheek, Don Benito
med to have even less welcome for the breeze than the calm.

Poor fellow, thought Captain Delano, bitter experience has taught him that
e ripple does not make a wind, any more than one swallow a summer. But he
mistaken for once. I will get his ship in for him, and prove it.

Briefly alluding to his weak condition, he urged his host to remain quietly
ere he was, since he (Captain Delano) would with pleasure take upon
mself the responsibility of making the best use of the wind.

Upon gaining the deck, Captain Delano started at the unexpected figure of
fal, monumentally fixed at the threshold, like one of those sculptured
ters of black marble guarding the porches of Egyptian tombs.

But this time the start was, perhaps, purely physical. Atufal's presence,
gularly attesting docility even in sullenness, was contrasted with that of the
chet-polishers, who in patience evinced their industry; while both spectacles
owed, that lax as Don Benito's general authority might be, still, whenever he
ose to exert it, no man so savage or colossal but must, more or less, bow.

Snatching a trumpet which hung from the bulwarks, with a free step Captain
lano advanced to the forward edge of the poop, issuing his orders in his best
anish. The few sailors and many Negroes, all equally pleased, obediently set
out heading the ship toward the harbour.

While giving some directions about setting a lower stu'n'-sail, suddenly
otain Delano heard a voice faithfully repeating his orders. Turning, he saw
bo, now for the time acting, under the pilot, his original part of captain of the
ves. This assistance proved valuable. Tattered sails and warped yards were
on brought into some trim. And no brace or halyard was pulled but to the
the songs of the inspirited Negroes.

Good fellows, thought Captain Delano, a little training would make fine
lors of them. Why see, the very women pull and sing, too. These must be
ne of those Ashantee Negresses that make such capital soldiers, I've heard.
t who's at the helm? I must have a good hand there.

He went to see.

The San Dominick steered with a cumbrous tiller, with large horizontal
lleys attached. At each pulley-end stood a subordinate black, and between
m, at the tiller-head, the responsible post, a Spanish seaman, whose
untenance evinced his due share in the general hopefulness and confidence
the coming of the breeze.

He proved the same man who had behaved with so shamefaced an air on the
ndlass.

"Ah,- it is you, my man," exclaimed Captain Delano- "well, no more sheep's eyes now;- look straight forward and keep the ship so. Good hand, I trust? An want to get into the harbour, don't you?"

"Si Senor," assented the man with an inward chuckle, grasping the tiller-he firmly. Upon this, unperceived by the American, the two blacks eyed the sailo askance.

Finding all right at the helm, the pilot went forward to the forecastle, to se how matters stood there.

The ship now had way enough to breast the current. With the approach of evening, the breeze would be sure to freshen.

Having done all that was needed for the present, Captain Delano, giving his last orders to the sailors, turned aft to report affairs to Don Benito in the cabi perhaps additionally incited to rejoin him by the hope of snatching a moment private chat while his servant was engaged upon deck.

From opposite sides, there were, beneath the poop, two approaches to the cabin; one further forward than the other, and consequently communicating with a longer passage. Marking the servant still above, Captain Delano, taking the nighest entrance- the one last named, and at whose porch Atufal still stoo hurried on his way, till, arrived at the cabin threshold, he paused an instant, a little to recover from his eagerness. Then, with the words of his intended business upon his lips, he entered. As he advanced toward the Spaniard, on th transom, he heard another footstep, keeping time with his. From the opposite door, a salver in hand, the servant was likewise advancing.

"Confound the faithful fellow," thought Captain Delano; "what a vexatious coincidence."

Possibly, the vexation might have been something different, were it not for the buoyant confidence inspired by the breeze. But even as it was, he felt a slight twinge, from a sudden involuntary association in his mind of Babo with Atufal.

"Don Benito," said he, "I give you joy; the breeze will hold, and will increas By the way, your tall man and time-piece, Atufal, stands without. By your ord of course?"

Don Benito recoiled, as if at some bland satirical touch, delivered with such adroit garnish of apparent good-breeding as to present no handle for retort.

He is like one flayed alive, thought Captain Delano; where may one touch h without causing a shrink?

The servant moved before his master, adjusting a cushion; recalled to civili the Spaniard stiffly replied: "You are right. The slave appears where you saw

1, according to my command; which is, that if at the given hour I am below,
must take his stand and abide my coming."

Ah now, pardon me, but that is treating the poor fellow like an ex-king
ied. Ah, Don Benito," smiling, "for all the license you permit in some things, I
r lest, at bottom, you are a bitter hard master."

Again Don Benito shrank; and this time, as the good sailor thought, from a
uine twinge of his conscience.

Conversation now became constrained. In vain Captain Delano called
ention to the now perceptible motion of the keel gently cleaving the sea; with
k-lustre eye, Don Benito returned words few and reserved.

By-and-by, the wind having steadily risen, and still blowing right into the
bour, bore the San Dominick swiftly on. Rounding a point of land, the sealer
distance came into open view.

Meantime Captain Delano had again repaired to the deck, remaining there
ne time. Having at last altered the ship's course, so as to give the reef a wide
th, he returned for a few moments below.

will cheer up my poor friend, this time, thought he.

"Better and better, Don Benito," he cried as he blithely re-entered; "there will
n be an end to your cares, at least for awhile. For when, after a long, sad
age, you know, the anchor drops into the haven, all its vast weight seems
ed from the captain's heart. We are getting on famously, Don Benito. My ship
n sight. Look through this side-light here; there she is; all a-taunt-o! The
:helor's Delight, my good friend. Ah, how this wind braces one up. Come, you
st take a cup of coffee with me this evening. My old steward will give you as
e a cup as ever any sultan tasted. What say you, Don Benito, will you?"

At first, the Spaniard glanced feverishly up, casting a longing look toward the
ler, while with mute concern his servant gazed into his face. Suddenly the
ague of coldness returned, and dropping back to his cushions he was silent.

"You do not answer. Come, all day you have been my host; would you have
spitality all on one side?"

"I cannot go," was the response.

"What? it will not fatigue you. The ships will lie together as near as they can,
hout swinging foul. It will be little more than stepping from deck to deck;
ich is but as from room to room. Come, come, you must not refuse me."

"I cannot go," decisively and repulsively repeated Don Benito.

Renouncing all but the last appearance of courtesy, with a sort of cadaverous
lenness, and biting his thin nails to the quick, he glanced, almost glared, at

his guest; as if impatient that a stranger's presence should interfere with the full indulgence of his morbid hour. Meantime the sound of the parted waters came more and more gurglingly and merrily in at the windows; as reproaching him for his dark spleen; as telling him that, sulk as he might, and go mad with, nature cared not a jot; since, whose fault was it, pray? But the foul mood was now at its depth, as the fair wind at its height.

There was something in the man so far beyond any mere unsociality or sourness previously evinced, that even the forbearing good-nature of his guest could no longer endure it. Wholly at a loss to account for such demeanour, and deeming sickness with eccentricity, however extreme, no adequate excuse, who satisfied, too, that nothing in his own conduct could justify it, Captain Delano's pride began to be roused. Himself became reserved. But all seemed one to the Spaniard. Quitting him, therefore, Captain Delano once more went to the deck.

The ship was now within less than two miles of the sealer. The whale-boat was seen darting over the interval.

To be brief, the two vessels, thanks to the pilot's skill, ere long in neighbour style lay anchored together.

Before returning to his own vessel, Captain Delano had intended communicating to Don Benito the practical details of the proposed services to be rendered. But, as it was, unwilling anew to subject himself to rebuffs, he resolved, now that he had seen the San Dominick safely moored, immediately quit her, without further allusion to hospitality or business. Indefinitely postponing his ulterior plans, he would regulate his future actions according future circumstances. His boat was ready to receive him; but his host still tarried below. Well, thought Captain Delano, if he has little breeding, the more need to show mine. He descended to the cabin to bid a ceremonious, and, it may be, tacitly rebukeful adieu. But to his great satisfaction, Don Benito, as if he began to feel the weight of that treatment with which his slighted guest had, indecorously, retaliated upon him, now supported by his servant, rose to his feet, and grasping Captain Delano's hand, stood tremulous; too much agitated speak. But the good augury hence drawn was suddenly dashed, by his resuming all his previous reserve, with augmented gloom, as, with half-averted eyes, he silently reseated himself on his cushions. With a corresponding return of his own chilled feelings, Captain Delano bowed and withdrew.

He was hardly midway in the narrow corridor, dim as a tunnel, leading from the cabin to the stairs, when a sound, as of the tolling for execution in some jail yard, fell on his ears. It was the echo of the ship's flawed bell, striking the hour drearily reverberated in this subterranean vault. Instantly, by a fatality not to be withstood, his mind, responsive to the portent, swarmed with superstitious suspicions. He paused. In images far swifter than these sentences, the minute details of all his former distrusts swept through him.

48

litherto, credulous good-nature had been too ready to furnish excuses for
sonable fears. Why was the Spaniard, so superfluously punctilious at times,
v heedless of common propriety in not accompanying to the side his
arting guest? Did indisposition forbid? Indisposition had not forbidden
re irksome exertion that day. His last equivocal demeanour recurred. He had
:n to his feet, grasped his guest's hand, motioned toward his hat; then, in an
:ant, all was eclipsed in sinister muteness and gloom. Did this imply one
:f, repentant relenting at the final moment, from some iniquitous plot,
owed by remorseless return to it? His last glance seemed to express a
amitous, yet acquiescent farewell to Captain Delano for ever. Why decline
invitation to visit the sealer that evening? Or was the Spaniard less
dened than the Jew, who refrained not from supping at the board of him
om the same night he meant to betray? What imported all those day-long
gmas and contradictions, except they were intended to mystify, preliminary
ome stealthy blow? Atufal, the pretended rebel, but punctual shadow, that
ment lurked by the threshold without. He seemed a sentry, and more. Who,
nis own confession, had stationed him there? Was the Negro now lying in
t?

he Spaniard behind- his creature before: to rush from darkness to light was
involuntary choice.

he next moment, with clenched jaw and hand, he passed Atufal, and stood
irmed in the light. As he saw his trim ship lying peacefully at her anchor, and
ost within ordinary call; as he saw his household boat, with familiar faces in
atiently rising and falling on the short waves by the San Dominick's side;
l then, glancing about the decks where he stood, saw the oakum-pickers still
vely plying their fingers; and heard the low, buzzing whistle and industrious
n of the hatchet-polishers, still bestirring themselves over their endless
upation; and more than all, as he saw the benign aspect of Nature, taking her
ocent repose in the evening; the screened sun in the quiet camp of the west
ning out like the mild light from Abraham's tent; as his charmed eye and ear
k in all these, with the chained figure of the black, the clenched jaw and hand
ixed. Once again he smiled at the phantoms which had mocked him, and felt
1ething like a tinge of remorse, that, by indulging them even for a moment,
should, by implication, have betrayed an almost atheistic doubt of the ever-
tchful Providence above.

here was a few minutes' delay, while, in obedience to his orders, the boat
s being hooked along to the gangway. During this interval, a sort of saddened
isfaction stole over Captain Delano, at thinking of the kindly offices he had
t day discharged for a stranger. Ah, thought he, after good actions one's
iscience is never ungrateful, however much so the benefited party may be.

Presently, his foot, in the first act of descent into the boat, pressed the first round of the side-ladder, his face presented inward upon the deck. In the same moment, he heard his name courteously sounded; and, to his pleased surprise saw Don Benito advancing- an unwonted energy in his air, as if, at the last moment, intent upon making amends for his recent discourtesy. With instinctive good feeling, Captain Delano, revoking his foot, turned and reciprocally advanced. As he did so, the Spaniard's nervous eagerness increased, but his vital energy failed; so that, the better to support him, the servant, placing his master's hand on his naked shoulder, and gently holding there, formed himself into a sort of crutch.

When the two captains met, the Spaniard again fervently took the hand of American, at the same time casting an earnest glance into his eyes, but, as before, too much overcome to speak.

I have done him wrong, self-reproachfully thought Captain Delano; his apparent coldness has deceived me; in no instance has he meant to offend.

Meantime, as if fearful that the continuance of the scene might too much unstring his master, the servant seemed anxious to terminate it. And so, still presenting himself as a crutch, and walking between the two captains, he advanced with them toward the gangway; while still, as if full of kindly contrition, Don Benito would not let go the hand of Captain Delano, but retain it in his, across the black's body.

Soon they were standing by the side, looking over into the boat, whose cre turned up their curious eyes. Waiting a moment for the Spaniard to relinquish his hold, the now embarrassed Captain Delano lifted his foot, to overstep the threshold of the open gangway; but still Don Benito would not let go his hand And yet, with an agitated tone, he said, "I can go no further; here I must bid y adieu. Adieu, my dear, dear Don Amasa. Go- go!" suddenly tearing his hand loose, "go, and God guard you better than me, my best friend."

Not unaffected, Captain Delano would now have lingered; but catching the meekly admonitory eye of the servant, with a hasty farewell he descended in his boat, followed by the continual adieus of Don Benito, standing rooted in tl gangway.

Seating himself in the stern, Captain Delano, making a last salute, ordered boat shoved off. The crew had their oars on end. The bowsman pushed the bc a sufficient distance for the oars to be lengthwise dropped. The instant that v done, Don Benito sprang over the bulwarks, falling at the feet of Captain Delano; at the same time, calling towards his ship, but in tones so frenzied, th none in the boat could understand him. But, as if not equally obtuse, three Spanish sailors, from three different and distant parts of the ship, splashed in the sea, swimming after their captain, as if intent upon his rescue.

The dismayed officer of the boat eagerly asked what this meant. To which, ?tain Delano, turning a disdainful smile upon the unaccountable Benito ?eno, answered that, for his part, he neither knew nor cared; but it seemed as ?e Spaniard had taken it into his head to produce the impression among his ?ple that the boat wanted to kidnap him. "Or else- give way for your lives," he ?dly added, starting at a clattering hubbub in the ship, above which rang the ?sin of the hatchet-polishers; and seizing Don Benito by the throat he added, ?is plotting pirate means murder!" Here, in apparent verification of the ?rds, the servant, a dagger in his hand, was seen on the rail overhead, poised, ?he act of leaping, as if with desperate fidelity to befriend his master to the ?t; while, seemingly to aid the black, the three Spanish sailors were trying to ?mber into the hampered bow. Meantime, the whole host of Negroes, as if ?amed at the sight of their jeopardized captain, impended in one sooty ?lanche over the bulwarks.

?ll this, with what preceded, and what followed, occurred with such ?olutions of rapidity, that past, present, and future seemed one.

?eeing the Negro coming, Captain Delano had flung the Spaniard aside, ?ost in the very act of clutching him, and, by the unconscious recoil, shifting ? place, with arms thrown up, so promptly grappled the servant in his ?cent, that with dagger presented at Captain Delano's heart, the black seemed ?urpose to have leaped there as to his mark. But the weapon was wrenched ?ay, and the assailant dashed down into the bottom of the boat, which now, ?h disentangled oars, began to speed through the sea.

?t this juncture, the left hand of Captain Delano, on one side, again clutched ? half-reclined Don Benito, heedless that he was in a speechless faint, while ?right foot, on the other side, ground the prostrate Negro; and his right arm ?ssed for added speed on the after oar, his eye bent forward, encouraging his ?n to their utmost.

?ut here, the officer of the boat, who had at last succeeded in beating off the ?ving Spanish sailors, and was now, with face turned aft, assisting the ?vsman at his oar, suddenly called to Captain Delano, to see what the black ?s about; while a Portuguese oarsman shouted to him to give heed to what the ?niard was saying.

?lancing down at his feet, Captain Delano saw the freed hand of the servant ?ing with a second dagger- a small one, before concealed in his wool- with ?s he was snakishly writhing up from the boat's bottom, at the heart of his ?ster, his countenance lividly vindictive, expressing the centred purpose of ? soul; while the Spaniard, half-choked, was vainly shrinking away, with ?sky words, incoherent to all but the Portuguese.

?hat moment, across the long benighted mind of Captain Delano, a flash of ?elation swept, illuminating in unanticipated clearness Benito Cereno's whole

51

mysterious demeanour, with every enigmatic event of the day, as well as the entire past voyage of the San Dominick. He smote Babo's hand down, but his own heart smote him harder. With infinite pity he withdrew his hold from Do Benito. Not Captain Delano, but Don Benito, the black, in leaping into the boat had intended to stab.

Both the black's hands were held, as, glancing up toward the San Dominick Captain Delano, now with the scales dropped from his eyes, saw the Negroes, not in misrule, not in tumult, not as if frantically concerned for Don Benito, but with mask torn away, flourishing hatchets and knives, in ferocious piratical revolt. Like delirious black dervishes, the six Ashantees danced on the poop. Prevented by their foes from springing into the water, the Spanish boys were hurrying up to the topmost spars, while such of the few Spanish sailors, not already in the sea, less alert, were descried, helplessly mixed in, on deck, with the blacks.

Meantime Captain Delano hailed his own vessel, ordering the ports up, and the guns run out. But by this time the cable of the San Dominick had been cut and the fag-end, in lashing out, whipped away the canvas shroud about the beak, suddenly revealing, as the bleached hull swung round toward the open ocean, death for the figurehead, in a human skeleton; chalky comment on the chalked words below, "Follow your leader."

At the sight, Don Benito, covering his face, wailed out: "'Tis he, Aranda! my murdered, unburied friend!"

Upon reaching the sealer, calling for ropes, Captain Delano bound the Negr who made no resistance, and had him hoisted to the deck. He would then hav assisted the now almost helpless Don Benito up the side; but Don Benito, war as he was, refused to move, or be moved, until the Negro should have been fir put below out of view. When, presently assured that it was done, he no more shrank from the ascent.

The boat was immediately despatched back to pick up the three swimming sailors. Meantime, the guns were in readiness, though, owing to the San Dominick having glided somewhat astern of the sealer, only the aftermost on could be brought to bear. With this, they fired six times; thinking to cripple th fugitive ship by bringing down her spars. But only a few inconsiderable ropes were shot away. Soon the ship was beyond the guns' range, steering broad ou of the bay; the blacks thickly clustering round the bowsprit, one moment with taunting cries toward the whites, the next with up-thrown gestures hailing th now dusky expanse of ocean- cawing crows escaped from the hand of the fowler.

The first impulse was to slip the cables and give chase. But, upon second thought, to pursue with whale-boat and yawl seemed more promising.

Jpon inquiring of Don Benito what firearms they had on board the San
minick, Captain Delano was answered that they had none that could be used;
ause, in the earlier stages of the mutiny, a cabin-passenger, since dead, had
retly put out of order the locks of what few muskets there were. But with all
remaining strength, Don Benito entreated the American not to give chase,
 her with ship or boat; for the Negroes had already proved themselves such
peradoes, that, in case of a present assault, nothing but a total massacre of
whites could be looked for. But, regarding this warning as coming from one
ose spirit had been crushed by misery, the American did not give up his
ign.

he boats were got ready and armed. Captain Delano ordered twenty-five
n into them. He was going himself when Don Benito grasped his arm. "What!
e you saved my life, Senor, and are you now going to throw away your
n?"

he officers also, for reasons connected with their interests and those of the
age, and a duty owing to the owners, strongly objected against their
nmander's going. Weighing their remonstrances a moment, Captain Delano
bound to remain; appointing his chief mate- an athletic and resolute man,
o had been a privateer's man, and, as his enemies whispered, a pirate- to
id the party. The more to encourage the sailors, they were told, that the
inish captain considered his ship as good as lost; that she and her cargo,
luding some gold and silver, were worth upwards of ten thousand
ibloons. Take her, and no small part should be theirs. The sailors replied
h a shout.

he fugitives had now almost gained an offing. It was nearly night; but the
on was rising. After hard, prolonged pulling, the boats came up on the ship's
arters, at a suitable distance laying upon their oars to discharge their
skets. Having no bullets to return, the Negroes sent their yells. But, upon the
ond volley, Indian-like, they hurtled their hatchets. One took off a sailor's
gers. Another struck the whale-boat's bow, cutting off the rope there, and
naining stuck in the gunwale, like a woodman's axe. Snatching it, quivering
m its lodgment, the mate hurled it back. The returned gauntlet now stuck in
ship's broken quarter-gallery, and so remained.

he Negroes giving too hot a reception, the whites kept a more respectful
tance. Hovering now just out of reach of the hurtling hatchets, they, with a
w to the close encounter which must soon come, sought to decoy the blacks
o entirely disarming themselves of their most murderous weapons in a
id-to-hand fight, by foolishly flinging them, as missiles, short of the mark,
o the sea. But ere long perceiving the stratagem, the Negroes desisted,
ough not before many of them had to replace their lost hatchets with

53

handspikes; an exchange which, as counted upon, proved in the end favourabl
to the assailants.

Meantime, with a strong wind, the ship still clove the water; the boats
alternately falling behind, and pulling up, to discharge fresh volleys.

The fire was mostly directed toward the stern, since there, chiefly, the
Negroes, at present, were clustering. But to kill or maim the Negroes was not
the object. To take them, with the ship, was the object. To do it, the ship must
boarded; which could not be done by boats while she was sailing so fast.

A thought now struck the mate. Observing the Spanish boys still aloft, high
they could get, he called to them to descend to the yards, and cut adrift the sa
It was done. About this time, owing to causes hereafter to be shown, two
Spaniards, in the dress of sailors and conspicuously showing themselves, wer
killed; not by volleys, but by deliberate marksman's shots; while, as it
afterwards appeared, during one of the general discharges, Atufal, the black,
and the Spaniard at the helm likewise were killed. What now, with the loss of
the sails, and loss of leaders, the ship became unmanageable to the Negroes.

With creaking masts she came heavily round to the wind; the prow slowly
swinging into view of the boats, its skeleton gleaming in the horizontal
moonlight, and casting a gigantic ribbed shadow upon the water. One extend
arm of the ghost seemed beckoning the whites to avenge it.

"Follow your leader!" cried the mate; and, one on each bow, the boats
boarded. Sealing-spears and cutlasses crossed hatchets and handspikes.
Huddled upon the long-boat amidships, the Negresses raised a wailing chant,
whose chorus was the clash of the steel.

For a time, the attack wavered; the Negroes wedging themselves to beat it
back; the half-repelled sailors, as yet unable to gain a footing, fighting as
troopers in the saddle, one leg sideways flung over the bulwarks, and one
without, plying their cutlasses like carters' whips. But in vain. They were alm
overborne, when, rallying themselves into a squad as one man, with a huzza,
they sprang inboard; where, entangled, they involuntarily separated again. F
a few breaths' space there was a vague, muffled, inner sound as of submerge
sword-fish rushing hither and thither through shoals of black-fish. Soon, in a
reunited band, and joined by the Spanish seamen, the whites came to the
surface, irresistibly driving the Negroes toward the stern. But a barricade of
casks and sacks, from side to side, had been thrown up by the mainmast. Her
the Negroes faced about, and though scorning peace or truce, yet fain would
have had a respite. But, without pause, overleaping the barrier, the unflaggin
sailors again closed. Exhausted, the blacks now fought in despair. Their red
tongues lolled, wolf-like, from their black mouths. But the pale sailors' teeth
were set; not a word was spoken; and, in five minutes more, the ship was wo

Nearly a score of the Negroes were killed. Exclusive of those by the balls, many were mangled; their wounds- mostly inflicted by the long-edged sealing-spears- resembling those shaven ones of the English at Preston Pans, made by the poled scythes of the Highlanders. On the other side, none were killed, though several were wounded; some severely, including the mate. The surviving Negroes were temporarily secured, and the ship, towed back into the harbour at midnight, once more lay anchored.

Omitting the incidents and arrangements ensuing, suffice it that, after two days spent in refitting, the two ships sailed in company for Concepcion in Chili, and thence for Lima in Peru; where, before the vice-regal courts, the whole affair, from the beginning, underwent investigation.

Though, midway on the passage, the ill-fated Spaniard, relaxed from constraint, showed some signs of regaining health with free-will; yet, agreeably to his own foreboding, shortly before arriving at Lima, he relapsed, finally becoming so reduced as to be carried ashore in arms. Hearing of his story and plight, one of the many religious institutions of the City of Kings opened an hospitable refuge to him, where both physician and priest were his nurses, and a member of the order volunteered to be his one special guardian and consoler, by night and by day.

The following extracts, translated from one of the official Spanish documents, will, it is hoped, shed light on the preceding narrative, as well as, in the first place, reveal the true port of departure and true history of the San Dominick's voyage, down to the time of her touching at the island of Santa Maria.

But, ere the extracts come, it may be well to preface them with a remark.

The document selected, from among many others, for partial translation, contains the deposition of Benito Cereno; the first taken in the case. Some disclosures therein were, at the time, held dubious for both learned and natural reasons. The tribunal inclined to the opinion that the deponent, not undisturbed in his mind by recent events, raved of some things which could never have happened. But subsequent depositions of the surviving sailors, bearing out the revelations of their captain in several of the strangest particulars, gave credence to the rest. So that the tribunal, in its final decision, rested its capital sentences upon statements which, had they lacked confirmation, it would have deemed it but duty to reject.

I, DON JOSE DE ABOS AND PADILLA, His Majesty's Notary for the Royal Revenue, and Register of this Province, and Notary Public of the Holy Crusade of this Bishopric, etc.

Do certify and declare, as much as is requisite in law, that, in the criminal case commenced the twenty-fourth of the month of September, in the year

seventeen hundred and ninety-nine, against the Senegal Negroes of the ship ?
Dominick, the following declaration before me was made.

Declaration of the first witness, DON BENITO CERENO.

The same day, and month, and year, His Honour, Doctor Juan Martinez de
Dozas, Councillor of the Royal Audience of this Kingdom, and learned in the l
of this Intendancy, ordered the captain of the ship San Dominick, Don Benito
Cereno, to appear; which he did in his litter, attended by the monk Infelez; of
whom he received, before Don Jose de Abos and Padilla, Notary Public of the
Holy Crusade, the oath, which he took by God, our Lord, and a sign of the Cro.
under which he promised to tell the truth of whatever he should know and
should be asked;- and being interrogated agreeably to the tenor of the act
commencing the process, he said, that on the twentieth of May last, he set sai
with his ship from the port of Valparaiso, bound to that of Callao; loaded with
the produce of the country and one hundred and sixty blacks, of both sexes,
mostly belonging to Don AlexandroAranda, gentleman, of the city of Mendoz;
that the crew of the ship consisted of thirty-six men, beside the persons who
went as passengers; that the Negroes were in part as follows:

*[Here, in the original, follows a list of some fifty names, descriptions, and age
compiled from certain recovered documents of Aranda's, and also from
recollections of the deponent, from which portions only are extracted.]*

-One, from about eighteen to nineteen years, named Jose, and this was the
man that waited upon his master, Don Alexandro, and who speaks well the
Spanish, having served him four or five years;... a mulatto, named Francesco,
cabin steward, of a good person and voice, having sung in the Valparaiso
churches, native of the province of Buenos Ayres, aged about thirty-five year.
A smart Negro, named Dago, who had been for many years a gravedigger
among the Spaniards, aged forty-six years.... Four old Negroes, born in Africa,
from sixty to seventy, but sound, caulkers by trade, whose names are as
follows:- the first was named Muri, and he was killed (as was also his son
named Diamelo); the second, Nacta; the third, Yola, likewise killed; the fourth
Ghofan; and six full-grown Negroes, aged from thirty to forty-five, all raw, an
born among the Ashantees- Martinqui, Yan, Lecbe, Mapenda, Yambaio, Akim;
four of whom were killed;... a powerful Negro named Atufal, who, being
supposed to have been a chief in Africa, his owners set great store by him.... A
a small Negro of Senegal, but some years among the Spaniards, aged about
thirty, which Negro's name was Babo;... that he does not remember the name
of the others, but that still expecting the residue of Don Alexandro's papers w
be found, will then take due account of them all, and remit to the court;... and
thirty-nine women and children of all ages.

[After the catalogue, the deposition goes on as follows:]

..That all the Negroes slept upon deck, as is customary in this navigation, and
ae wore fetters, because the owner, his friend Aranda, told him that they
re all tractable;... that on the seventh day after leaving port, at three o'clock
he morning, all the Spaniards being asleep except the two officers on the
tch, who were the boatswain, Juan Robles, and the carpenter, Juan Bautista
vete, and the helmsman and his boy, the Negroes revolted suddenly,
unded dangerously the boatswain and the carpenter, and successively killed
hteen men of those who were sleeping upon deck, some with handspikes
l hatchets, and others by throwing them alive overboard, after tying them;
t of the Spaniards upon deck, they left about seven, as he thinks, alive and
l, to manoeuvre the ship, and three or four more who hid themselves
nained also alive. Although in the act of revolt the Negroes made themselves
sters of the hatchway, six or seven wounded went through it to the cockpit,
hout any hindrance on their part; that in the act of revolt, the mate and
ther person, whose name he does not recollect, attempted to come up
ough the hatchway, but having been wounded at the onset, they were
iged to return to the cabin; that the deponent resolved at break of day to
ne up the companionway, where the Negro Babo was, being the ringleader,
l Atufal, who assisted him, and having spoken to them, exhorted them to
se committing such atrocities, asking them, at the same time, what they
nted and intended to do, offering, himself, to obey their commands; that,
withstanding this, they threw, in his presence, three men, alive and tied,
erboard; that they told the deponent to come up, and that they would not kill
1; which having done, the Negro Babo asked him whether there were in
se seas any Negro countries where they might be carried, and he answered
m, No, that the Negro Babo afterwards told him to carry them to Senegal, or
he neighbouring islands of St. Nicholas; and he answered, that this was
possible, on account of the great distance, the necessity involved of rounding
e Horn, the bad condition of the vessel, the want of provisions, sails, and
ter; but that the Negro Babo replied to him he must carry them in any way;
t they would do and conform themselves to everything the deponent should
juire as to eating and drinking; that after a long conference, being absolutely
npelled to please them, for they threatened him to kill all the whites if they
re not, at all events, carried to Senegal, he told them that what was most
nting for the voyage was water; that they would go near the coast to take it,
l hence they would proceed on their course; that the Negro Babo agreed to
and the deponent steered toward the intermediate ports, hoping to meet
ne Spanish or foreign vessel that would save them; that within ten or eleven
/s they saw the land, and continued their course by it in the vicinity of Nasca;
t the deponent observed that the Negroes were now restless and mutinous,
:ause he did not effect the taking in of water, the Negro Babo having
juired, with threats, that it should be done, without fail, the following day; he
l him he saw plainly that the coast was steep, and the rivers designated in

the maps were not be found, with other reasons suitable to the circumstance: that the best way would be to go to the island of Santa Maria, where they mig water and victual easily, it being a desert island, as the foreigners did; that th deponent did not go to Pisco, that was near, nor make any other port of the coast, because the Negro Babo had intimated to him several times, that he would kill all the whites the very moment he should perceive any city, town, settlement of any kind on the shores to which they should be carried; that having determined to go to the island of Santa Maria, as the deponent had planned, for the purpose of trying whether, in the passage or in the island its they could find any vessel that should favour them, or whether he could escap from it in a boat to the neighbouring coast of Arruco; to adopt the necessary means he immediately changed his course, steering for the island; that the Negroes Babo and Atufal held daily conferences, in which they discussed wha was necessary for their design of returning to Senegal, whether they were to kill all the Spaniards, and particularly the deponent; that eight days after parting from the coast of Nasca, the deponent being on the watch a little after day-break, and soon after the Negroes had their meeting, the Negro Babo can to the place where the deponent was, and told him that he had determined to kill his master, Don AlexandroAranda, both because he and his companions could not otherwise be sure of their liberty, and that, to keep the seamen in subjection, he wanted to prepare a warning of what road they should be mad to take did they or any of them oppose him; and that, by means of the death o Don Alexandro, that warning would best be given; but, that what this last meant, the deponent did not at the time comprehend, nor could not, further than that the death of Don Alexandro was intended; and moreover, the Negro Babo proposed to the deponent to call the mate Raneds, who was sleeping in the cabin, before the thing was done, for fear, as the deponent understood it, that the mate, who was a good navigator, should be killed with Don Alexandr and the rest; that the deponent, who was the friend, from youth of Don Alexandro, prayed and conjured, but all was useless; for the Negro Babo answered him that the thing could not be prevented, and that all the Spaniar risked their death if they should attempt to frustrate his will in this matter, o any other; that, in this conflict, the deponent called the mate, Raneds, who wa forced to go apart, and immediately the Negro Babo commanded the AshanteeMartinqui and the AshanteeLecbe to go and commit the murder; tha those two went down with hatchets to the berth of Don Alexandro; that, yet h alive and mangled, they dragged him on deck; that they were going to throw him overboard in that state, but the Negro Babo stopped them, bidding the murder be completed on the deck before him, which was done, when, by his orders, the body was carried below, forward; that nothing more was seen of i by the deponent for three days;... that Don Alonzo Sidonia, an old man, long resident at Valparaiso, and lately appointed to a civil office in Peru, whither h had taken passage, was at the time sleeping in the berth opposite Don

xandro's; that, awakening at his cries, surprised by them, and at the sight of
  Negroes with their bloody hatchets in their hands, he threw himself into the
  through a window which was near him, and was drowned, without it being
  he power of the deponent to assist or take him up;... that, a short time after
ing Aranda, they brought upon deck his german-cousin, of middle-age, Don
ncisco Masa, of Mendoza, and the young Don Joaquin, Marques de
mboalaza, then lately from Spain, with his Spanish servant Ponce, and the
ee young clerks of Aranda, Jose Mozairi, Lorenzo Bargas, and
rmenegildoGandix, all of Cadiz; that Don Joaquin and HermenegildoGandix,
  Negro Babo for purposes hereafter to appear, preserved alive; but Don
ncisco Masa, Jose Mozairi, and Lorenzo Bargas, with Ponce, the servant,
ide the boatswain, Juan Robles, the boatswain's mates, Manuel Viscaya and
lerigoHurta, and, four of the sailors, the Negro Babo ordered to be thrown
e into the sea, although they made no resistance, nor begged for anything
but mercy; that the boatswain, Juan Robles, who knew how to swim, kept
longest above water, making acts of contrition, and, in the last words he
ered, charged this deponent to cause mass to be said for his soul to our Lady
uccour;... that, during the three days which followed, the deponent,
ertain what fate had befallen the remains of Don Alexandro, frequently
ed the Negro Babo where they were, and, if still on board, whether they
re to be preserved for interment ashore, entreating him so to order it; that
  Negro Babo answered nothing till the fourth day, when at sunrise, the
ponent coming on deck, the Negro Babo showed him a skeleton, which had
n substituted for the ship's proper figure-head, the image of Christopher
on, the discoverer of the New World; that the Negro Babo asked him whose
leton that was, and whether, from its whiteness, he should not think it a
ite's; that, upon his covering his face, the Negro Babo, coming close, said
rds to this effect: "Keep faith with the blacks from here to Senegal, or you
ll in spirit, as now in body, follow your leader," pointing to the prow;... that
  same morning the Negro Babo took by succession each Spaniard forward,
l asked him whose skeleton that was, and whether, from its whiteness, he
uld not think it a white's; that each Spaniard covered his face; that then to
h the Negro Babo repeated the words in the first place said to the
ponent;... that they (the Spaniards), being then assembled aft, the Negro Babo
angued them, saying that he had now done all; that the deponent (as
igator for the Negroes) might pursue his course, warning him and all of
m that they should, soul and body, go the way of Don Alexandro if he saw
m (the Spaniards) speak or plot anything against them (the Negroes)- a
eat which was repeated every day; that, before the events last mentioned,
y had tied the cook to throw him overboard, for it is not known what thing
y heard him speak, but finally the Negro Babo spared his life, at the request
he deponent; that a few days after, the deponent, endeavouring not to omit
means to preserve the lives of the remaining whites, spoke to the Negroes

peace and tranquillity, and agreed to draw up a paper, signed by the deponer and the sailors who could write, as also by the Negro Babo, for himself and al the blacks, in which the deponent obliged himself to carry them to Senegal, a they not to kill any more, and he formally to make over to them the ship, with the cargo, with which they were for that time satisfied and quieted.... But the next day, the more surely to guard against the sailors' escape, the Negro Bab commanded all the boats to be destroyed but the long-boat, which was unseaworthy, and another, a cutter in good condition, which, knowing it wou yet be wanted for lowering the water casks, he had it lowered down into the hold.

[Various particulars of the prolonged and perplexed navigation ensuing here follow, with incidents of a calamitous calm, from which portion one passage is extracted, to wit:]

-That on the fifth day of the calm, all on board suffering much from the hea and want of water, and five having died in fits, and mad, the Negroes became irritable, and for a chance gesture, which they deemed suspicious- though it was harmless- made by the mate, Raneds, to the deponent, in the act of handi a quadrant, they killed him; but that for this they afterwards were sorry, the mate being the only remaining navigator on board, except the deponent.

-That omitting other events, which daily happened, and which can only ser uselessly to recall past misfortunes and conflicts, after seventy-three days' navigation, reckoned from the time they sailed from Nasca, during which the navigated under a scanty allowance of water, and were afflicted with the caln before mentioned, they at last arrived at the island of Santa Maria, on the seventeenth of the month of August, at about six o'clock in the afternoon, at which hour they cast anchor very near the American ship, Bachelor's Delight, which lay in the same bay, commanded by the generous Captain Amasa Delar but at six o'clock in the morning, they had already descried the port, and the Negroes became uneasy, as soon as at distance they saw the ship, not having expected to see one there; that the Negro Babo pacified them, assuring them that no fear need be had; that straightway he ordered the figure on the bow t be covered with canvas, as for repairs, and had the decks a little set in order; that for a time the Negro Babo and the Negro Atufal conferred; that the Negr Atufal was for sailing away, but the Negro Babo would not, and, by himself, ca about what to do; that at last he came to the deponent, proposing to him to sa and do all that the deponent declares to have said and done to the American captain;... that the Negro Babo warned him that if he varied in the least, or uttered any word, or gave any look that should give the least intimation of the past events or present state, he would instantly kill him, with all his companions, showing a dagger, which he carried hid, saying something which as he understood it, meant that that dagger would be alert as his eye; that the Negro Babo then announced the plan to all his companions, which pleased

m; that he then, the better to disguise the truth, devised many expedients, in
ne of them uniting deceit and defence; that of this sort was the device of the
Ashantees before named, who were his bravos; that them he stationed on
 break of the poop, as if to clean certain hatchets (in cases, which were part
he cargo), but in reality to use them, and distribute them at need, and at a
en word he told them that, among other devices, was the device of
senting Atufal, his right-hand man, as chained, though in a moment the
ins could be dropped; that in every particular he informed the deponent
at part he was expected to enact in every device, and what story he was to
on every occasion, always threatening him with instant death if he varied in
least; that, conscious that many of the Negroes would be turbulent, the
gro Babo appointed the four aged Negroes, who were caulkers, to keep what
nestic order they could on the decks; that again and again he harangued the
aniards and his companions, informing them of his intent, and of his devices,
l of the invented story that this deponent was to tell, charging them lest any
hem varied from that story; that these arrangements were made and
tured during the interval of two or three hours, between their first sighting
 ship and the arrival on board of Captain Amasa Delano; that this happened
about half-past seven in the morning, Captain Amasa Delano coming in his
at, and all gladly receiving him; that the deponent, as well as he could force
iself, acting then the part of principal owner, and a free captain of the ship,
l Captain Amasa Delano, when called upon, that he came from Buenos Ayres,
und to Lima, with three hundred Negroes; that off Cape Horn, and in a
·sequent fever, many Negroes had died; that also, by similar casualties, all
 sea officers and the greatest part of the crew had died.

*And so the deposition goes on, circumstantially recounting the fictitious story
tated to the deponent by Babo, and through the deponent imposed upon
otain Delano; and also recounting the friendly offers of Captain Delano, with
er things, but all of which is here omitted. After the fictitious, strange story,
, the deposition proceeds:]*

That the generous Captain Amasa Delano remained on board all the day, till
left the ship anchored at six o'clock in the evening, deponent speaking to him
rays of his pretended misfortunes, under the fore-mentioned principles,
hout having had it in his power to tell a single word, or give him the least
t, that he might know the truth and state of things; because the Negro Babo,
 forming the office of an officious servant with all the appearance of
·mission of the humble slave, did not leave the deponent one moment; that
; was in order to observe the deponent's actions and words, for the Negro
oo understands well the Spanish; and besides, there were thereabout some
ers who were constantly on the watch, and likewise understood the
inish;... that upon one occasion, while deponent was standing on the deck
iversing with Amasa Delano, by a secret sign the Negro Babo drew him (the

deponent) aside, the act appearing as if originating with the deponent; that then, he being drawn aside, the Negro Babo proposed to him to gain from Amasa Delano full particulars about his ship, and crew, and arms; that the deponent asked "For what?" that the Negro Babo answered he might conceiv that, grieved at the prospect of what might overtake the generous Captain Amasa Delano, the deponent at first refused to ask the desired questions, and used every argument to induce the Negro Babo to give up this new design; th the Negro Babo showed the point of his dagger; that, after the information ha been obtained, the Negro Babo again drew him aside, telling him that that ve night he (the deponent) would be captain of two ships instead of one, for tha great part of the American's ship's crew being to be absent fishing, the six Ashantees, without any one else, would easily take it; that at this time he said other things to the same purpose; that no entreaties availed; that before Ama Delano's coming on board, no hint had been given touching the capture of th American ship; that to prevent this project the deponent was powerless;... -th in some things his memory is confused, he cannot distinctly recall every ever -that as soon as they had cast anchor at six of the clock in the evening, as has before been stated, the American captain took leave to return to his vessel; th upon a sudden impulse, which the deponent believes to have come from God and his angels, he, after the farewell had been said, followed the generous Captain Amasa Delano as far as the gunwale, where he stayed, under the pretence of taking leave, until Amasa Delano should have been seated in his boat; that on shoving off, the deponent sprang from the gunwale, into the boa and fell into it, he knows not how, God guarding him; that-

[Here, in the original, follows the account of what further happened at the escape, and how the "San Dominick" was retaken, and of the passage to the coc including in the recital many expressions of "eternal gratitude" to the "generou Captain Amasa Delano." The deposition then proceeds with recapitulatory remarks, and a partial renumeration of the Negroes, making record of their individual part in the past events, with a view to furnishing, according to command of the court, the data whereon to found the criminal sentences to be pronounced. From this portion is the following:]

-That he believes that all the Negroes, though not in the first place knowin to the design of revolt, when it was accomplished, approved it.... That the Neg Jose, eighteen years old, and in the personal service of Don Alexandro, was th one who communicated the information to the Negro Babo, about the state o things in the cabin, before the revolt; that this is known, because, in the preceding midnight, he used to come from his berth, which was under his master's, in the cabin, to the deck where the ringleader and his associates we and had secret conversations with the Negro Babo, in which he was several times seen by the mate; that, one night, the mate drove him away twice;... tha this same Negro Jose, was the one who, without being commanded to do so b

Negro Babo, as Lecbe and Martinqui were, stabbed his master, Don
xandro, after he had been dragged half-lifeless to the deck;... that the mulatto
ward, Francesco, was of the first band of revolters, that he was, in all things,
creature and tool of the Negro Babo; that, to make his court, he, just before a
•ast in the cabin, proposed, to the Negro Babo, poisoning a dish for the
ierous Captain Amasa Delano; this is known and believed, because the
groes have said it; but that the Negro Babo, having another design, forbade
ncesco;... that the AshanteeLecbe was one of the worst of them; for that, on
day the ship was retaken, he assisted in the defence of her, with a hatchet in
h hand, with one of which he wounded, in the breast, the chief mate of
ıasa Delano, in the first act of boarding; this all knew; that, in sight of the
)onent, Lecbe struck, with a hatchet, Don Francisco Masa when, by the Negro
)o's orders, he was carrying him to throw him overboard, alive; beside
·ticipating in the murder, before mentioned, of Don AlexandroAranda, and
ers of the cabin-passengers; that, owing to the fury with which the
ıantees fought in the engagement with the boats, but this Lecbe and Yan
·vived; that Yan was bad as Lecbe; that Yan was the man who, by Babo's
ımmand, willingly prepared the skeleton of Don Alexandro, in a way the
groes afterwards told the deponent, but which he, so long as reason is left
ı, can never divulge; that Yan and Lecbe were the two who, in a calm by
ht, riveted the skeleton to the bow; this also the Negroes told him; that the
gro Babo was he who traced the inscription below it; that the Negro Babo
s the plotter from first to last; he ordered every murder, and was the helm
l keel of the revolt; that Atufal was his lieutenant in all; but Atufal, with his
n hand, committed no murder; nor did the Negro Babo;... that Atufal was
)t, being killed in the fight with the boats, ere boarding;... that the Negresses,
ıge, were knowing to the revolt, and testified themselves satisfied at the
ıth of their master, Don Alexandro; that, had the Negroes not restrained
·m, they would have tortured to death, instead of simply killing, the
ıniards slain by command of the Negro Babo; that the Negresses used their
ıost influence to have the deponent made away with; that, in the various acts
murder, they sang songs and danced- not gaily, but solemnly; and before the
gagement with the boats, as well as during the action, they sang melancholy
ıgs to the Negroes, and that this melancholy tone was more inflaming than a
ferent one would have been, and was so intended; that all this is believed,
:ause the Negroes have said it.

·That of the thirty-six men of the crew- exclusive of the passengers (all of
om are now dead), which the deponent had knowledge of- six only remained
·e, with four cabin-boys and ship-boys, not included with the crew;.... -that
· Negroes broke an arm of one of the cabin-boys and gave him strokes with
.chets.

[Then follow various random disclosures referring to various periods of time The following are extracted:]

-That during the presence of Captain Amasa Delano on board, some attemp were made by the sailors, and one by HermenegildoGandix, to convey hints t him of the true state of affairs; but that these attempts were ineffectual, owin to fear of incurring death, and furthermore owing to the devices which offere contradictions to the true state of affairs; as well as owing to the generosity a piety of Amasa Delano, incapable of sounding such wickedness;... that LuysGalgo, a sailor about sixty years of age, and formerly of the king's navy, v one of those who sought to convey tokens to Captain Amasa Delano; but his intent, though undiscovered, being suspected, he was, on a pretence, made to retire out of sight, and at last into the hold, and there was made away with. T the Negroes have since said;... that one of the ship-boys feeling, from Captain Amasa Delano's presence, some hopes of release, and not having enough prudence, dropped some chance-word respecting his expectations, which be overheard and understood by a slave-boy with whom he was eating at the tir the latter struck him on the head with a knife, inflicting a bad wound, but of which the boy is now healing; that likewise, not long before the ship was brought to anchor, one of the seamen, steering at the time, endangered himse by letting the blacks remark a certain unconscious hopeful expression in his countenance, arising from some cause similar to the above; but this sailor, by his heedful after conduct, escaped;... that these statements are made to show the court that from the beginning to the end of the revolt, it was impossible fc the deponent and his men to act otherwise than they did;... -that the third cle HermenegildoGandix, who before had been forced to live among the seamen, wearing a seaman's habit, and in all respects appearing to be one for the time he, Gandix, was killed by a musket-ball fired through a mistake from the American boats before boarding; having in his fright ran up the mizzen-riggi calling to the boats- "don't board," lest upon their boarding the Negroes shou kill him; that this inducing the Americans to believe he some way favoured th cause of the Negroes, they fired two balls at him, so that he fell wounded fron the rigging, and was drowned in the sea;... -that the young Don Joaquin, Marques de Aramboalaza, like HermenegildoGandix, the third clerk, was degraded to the office and appearance of a common seaman; that upon one occasion, when Don Joaquin shrank, the Negro Babo commanded the AshanteeLecbe to take tar and heat it, and pour it upon Don Joaquin's hands; that Don Joaquin was killed owing to another mistake of the Americans, but c impossible to be avoided, as upon the approach of the boats, Don Joaquin, wit a hatchet tied edge out and upright to his hand, was made by the Negroes to appear on the bulwarks; whereupon, seen with arms in his hands and in a questionable attitude, he was shot for a renegade seaman;... -that on the pers of Don Joaquin was found secreted a jewel, which, by papers that were discovered, proved to have been meant for the shrine of our Lady of Mercy in

64

ua; a votive offering, beforehand prepared and guarded, to attest his
titude, when he should have landed in Peru, his last destination, for the safe
iclusion of his entire voyage from Spain;... -that the jewel, with the other
ects of the late Don Joaquin, is in the custody of the brethren of the Hospital
Sacerdotes, awaiting the decision of the honourable court;... -that, owing to
 condition of the deponent, as well as the haste in which the boats departed
 the attack, the Americans were not forewarned that there were, among the
parent crew, a passenger and one of the clerks disguised by the Negro Babo;...
at, beside the Negroes killed in the action, some were killed after the capture
l re-anchoring at night, when shackled to the ring-bolts on deck; that these
ths were committed by the sailors, ere they could be prevented. That so
on as informed of it, Captain Amasa Delano used all his authority, and, in
rticular with his own hand, struck down Martinez Gola, who, having found a
or in the pocket of an old jacket of his, which one of the shackled Negroes
l on, was aiming it at the Negro's throat; that the noble Captain Amasa
ano also wrenched from the hand of Bartholomew Barlo, a dagger secreted
he time of the massacre of the whites, with which he was in the act of
bbing a shackled Negro, who, the same day, with another Negro, had thrown
1 down and jumped upon him;... that, for all the events, befalling through so
g a time, during which the ship was in the hands of the Negro Babo, he
not here give account; but that, what he has said is the most substantial of
at occurs to him at present, and is the truth under the oath which he has
en; which declaration he affirmed and ratified, after hearing it read to him.

He said that he is twenty-nine years of age, and broken in body and mind;
t when finally dismissed by the court, he shall not return home to Chili, but
ake himself to the monastery on Mount Agonia without; and signed with his
nour, and crossed himself, and, for the time, departed as he came, in his litter,
h the monk Infelez, to the Hospital de Sacerdotes.

BENITO CERENO.

DOCTOR ROZAS.

f the deposition of Benito Cereno has served as the key to fit into the lock of
 complications which preceded it, then, as a vault whose door has been flung
:k, the San Dominick's hull lies open to-day.

Hitherto the nature of this narrative, besides rendering the intricacies in the
ginning unavoidable, has more or less required that many things, instead of
ng set down in the order of occurrence, should be retrospectively, or
egularly given; this last is the case with the following passages, which will
iclude the account:

During the long, mild voyage to Lima, there was, as before hinted, a period
ring which Don Benito a little recovered his health, or, at least in some
gree, his tranquillity. Ere the decided relapse which came, the two captains

had many cordial conversations- their fraternal unreserve in singular contra:
with former withdrawments.

Again and again, it was repeated, how hard it had been to enact the part
forced on the Spaniard by Babo.

"Ah, my dear Don Amasa," Don Benito once said, "at those very times whe
you thought me so morose and ungrateful- nay when, as you now admit, you
half thought me plotting your murder- at those very times my heart was froz
I could not look at you, thinking of what, both on board this ship and your ov
hung, from other hands, over my kind benefactor. And as God lives, Don Ama
I know not whether desire for my own safety alone could have nerved me to
that leap into your boat, had it not been for the thought that, did you,
unenlightened, return to your ship, you, my best friend, with all who might b
with you, stolen upon, that night, in your hammocks, would never in this wor
have wakened again. Do but think how you walked this deck, how you sat in
this cabin, every inch of ground mined into honey-combs under you. Had I
dropped the least hint, made the least advance toward an understanding
between us, death, explosive death- yours as mine- would have ended the
scene."

"True, true," cried Captain Delano, starting, "you saved my life, Don Benito
more than I yours; saved it, too, against my knowledge and will."

"Nay, my friend," rejoined the Spaniard, courteous even to the point of
religion, "God charmed your life, but you saved mine. To think of some things
you did- those smilings and chattings, rash pointings and gesturings. For less
than these, they slew my mate, Raneds; but you had the Prince of Heaven's sa
conduct through all ambuscades."

"Yes, all is owing to Providence, I know; but the temper of my mind that
morning was more than commonly pleasant, while the sight of so much
suffering- more apparent than real- added to my good nature, compassion, ai
charity, happily interweaving the three. Had it been otherwise, doubtless, as
you hint, some of my interferences with the blacks might have ended unhapp
enough. Besides that, those feelings I spoke of enabled me to get the better of
momentary distrust, at times when acuteness might have cost me my life,
without saving another's. Only at the end did my suspicions get the better of
me, and you know how wide of the mark they then proved."

"Wide, indeed," said Don Benito, sadly; "you were with me all day; stood w
me, sat with me, talked with me, looked at me, ate with me, drank with me; ai
yet, your last act was to clutch for a villain, not only an innocent man, but the
most pitiable of all men. To such degree may malign machinations and
deceptions impose. So far may even the best men err, in judging the conduct (
one with the recesses of whose condition he is not acquainted. But you were

66

ced to it; and you were in time undeceived. Would that, in both respects, it s so ever, and with all men."

I think I understand you; you generalize, Don Benito; and mournfully ough. But the past is passed; why moralize upon it? Forget it. See, yon bright has forgotten it all, and the blue sea, and the blue sky; these have turned r new leaves."

Because they have no memory," he dejectedly replied; "because they are not man."

But these mild trades that now fan your cheek, Don Benito, do they not ne with a human-like healing to you? Warm friends, steadfast friends are the des."

With their steadfastness they but waft me to my tomb, Senor," was the eboding response.

You are saved, Don Benito," cried Captain Delano, more and more onished and pained; "you are saved; what has cast such a shadow upon ?"

The Negro."

There was silence, while the moody man sat, slowly and unconsciously hering his mantle about him, as if it were a pall.

There was no more conversation that day.

But if the Spaniard's melancholy sometimes ended in muteness upon topics the above, there were others upon which he never spoke at all; on which, eed, all his old reserves were piled. Pass over the worst and, only to cidate, let an item or two of these be cited. The dress so precise and costly, rn by him on the day whose events have been narrated, had not willingly n put on. And that silver-mounted sword, apparent symbol of despotic nmand, was not, indeed, a sword, but the ghost of one. The scabbard, ificially stiffened, was empty.

As for the black- whose brain, not body, had schemed and led the revolt, with plot- his slight frame, inadequate to that which it held, had at once yielded he superior muscular strength of his captor, in the boat. Seeing all was over, uttered no sound, and could not be forced to. His aspect seemed to say: since nnot do deeds, I will not speak words. Put in irons in the hold, with the rest, was carried to Lima. During the passage Don Benito did not visit him. Nor n, nor at any time after, would he look at him. Before the tribunal he refused. en pressed by the judges he fainted. On the testimony of the sailors alone ted the legal identity of Babo. And yet the Spaniard would, upon occasion, bally refer to the Negro, as has been shown; but look on him he would not, could not.

Some months after, dragged to the gibbet at the tail of a mule, the black me his voiceless end. The body was burned to ashes; but for many days, the head that hive of subtlety, fixed on a pole in the Plaza, met, unabashed, the gaze of whites; and across the Plaza looked toward St. Bartholomew's church, in whe vaults slept then, as now, the recovered bones of Aranda; and across the Rim bridge looked toward the monastery, on Mount Agonia without; where, three months after being dismissed by the court, Benito Cereno, borne on the bier, did, indeed, follow his leader.

CPSIA information can be obtained
at www.ICGtesting.com
Printed in the USA
LVHW111938290520
656908LV00017B/702